CHLOROPHILIA

CRISTINA JURADO

T0343661

TRANSLATED BY
SUE BURKE

APEX BOOK COMPANY

Chlorophilia

ISBN (softcover) 978-1-955765-24-4

ISBN (epub) 978-1-955765-28-2

Cover art "Bracken" by Jana Heidersdorf

Cover design by Mikio Murikami

Translation from original Spanish by Sue Burke

Edited by Jason Sizemore and Rebecca Treasure

Visit us online at ApexBookCompany.com

First Edition: 2024

We're all mad here. I'm mad. You're mad.

How do you know I'm mad?

You must be, or you wouldn't have come here.

ALICE IN WONDERLAND (1865) BY LEWIS CARROLL

One person's craziness is another person's reality.

TIM BURTON

This story is a gift for Omar, who has always believed in my dreams.

CYCLOGENESIS

IT WAS BORN hungry with a craving so formidable, an urge to eat so unbearable that it could devour entire worlds and everything on them, alive or inert. The need to swallow anything in its path was engraved in its DNA as the very reason for its existence, to feed in order to continue to thunder. Anything it found would do, animate or inanimate. Swallow it whole, incorporate it, regurgitate it as tiny grains of reality, to descend over field and city, cover parks and peaks, slide over lakes and glaciers, rise over summits, and slip through canyons. To sweep the ground clean with its powerful breath, to clear all the trash that had grown on that big round rock, to purify the millions of nooks on that preposterous crust wandering through space without a pilot.

It emerged from Father Wind with his thousands of gales and whirlwinds, and from Mother Earth with her fertile mantle of sediments, in an impetuous copulation that became its first and only cradle. As befitted the child of such parents, its first act was to feed on them and launch itself into a maelstrom, exploring its surroundings, searching for nutrients. To probe, find, consume, absorb, and reclaim.

Because it was hard to live as heir to that perpetual hunger engraved into its molecules and haul the bulk that was its body through the twisted spaces of those preposterous places. Only with massive energy could it drag its troop of micro-soldiers from existential dust, as motes of reality, and send them forth to consume more elements. To excite them, it had to shake their senses and stimulate their wills with bursts of wind focused on carefully calculated points to sway them. To diminutive grains of limestone, it added bits of clay, silt, gravel, stones of every size, and small rocks, thus to digest whatever else remained. At times these granules nudged and caressed each other, at other times struck with mutually mutilating violence, wounding and tearing each other, provoking a sea of friction that molded new conscripts.

Why were those dominions so turbulent? Millions of obstacles appeared everywhere to complicate its task, slow its path, force it to attack every new structure, break each one down, and absorb it, investing a force that only made its voracious appetite grow. Anything small and lightweight was the first to fill the ranks of its army. These were all easy prey needing little to raise their mass into the air to be sundered. What they rendered was sweet but not as substantial as the stone buildings strewn across the ground, beautiful and sharp-edged, with hundreds of smaller morsels easily swallowed on the pulse of its airy lust.

Combing the water did not slake its thirst, instead, let it trace the valance of foam and delight in the cascades that drained from objects as they were raised from the depths. With pleasure it observed organic forms lose their vitality as it drew them down into the darkness, then emerge beautified by intricate red flowers on their skin. When it made them dance among the trammels emerging from the folds of the land, the flowers were less spectacular, their edges stunted and dirty.

And behind it all was the roar of the swarm that was its body, millions of shrieks drowning in the fleshy throats of minute beings, a beautiful song made from the spark that lit their lives and that, doused forever, wove the music of the dead. The intensity of that sound allowed it to extend its dominion across the entire planet, reaching the most remote confines and the places where temperatures kept life to a minimum. Its breath moistened the snows of the north and south, lubricating its shield of dust, and arousing its body of particles. It embraced deserts as only lovers know how, with lust and debauchery, tearing apart the dunes and absorbing the sand to continue lacerating the horizon.

It felt the continuous friction of its particles generating a sea of tension into which it sought to bathe the objects it found. Wasn't it a feast to embrace them? Didn't it redeem them by freeing them from the chains of their worldly existence? Why, then, did some resist?

When it believed that nothing could confront it, it encountered a series of pearls encrusted in the ground. These burnished domes defied it with lunatic obstinacy. Only those who had thrust their heads into the jaws of madness would dare to dream they could challenge it. What or who had made impregnable structures that resisted its advance? They intrigued it by their difference from constructions that had proliferated before its arrival, unable to offer true opposition. What distinguished these was that they seemed meant precisely to rebel against its power, and no matter how much it pummeled their spiteful, membrane-covered domes, it could find no chinks to slip through, no cracks in which to sink a claw. It threw itself against them with fury, unable to overcome their resistance. It tried vainly to distribute its vectors along the length of the flow of particles to blow them apart, its failure only making it more voracious.

It ached to savor what was hidden inside because concealment made its gluttony grow. It imagined the incredible delicacies awaiting its jaws, and as its craving swelled, so did the violence of its thrusts. Perhaps those exquisite morsels would finally sate its craving, fill the emptiness that never vanished, the desire that grew with each gust and squall.

Sometimes it managed to punch through, but the holes repaired themselves before it could launch its army through them. Every grain that formed its body—the splinters, pebbles, motes, and specks—explored the membranes and shared information with its peers, searching for weak points. They organized themselves into hordes of dust and sand, exquisitely synchronized whirlwinds, perfect storms of millions of grains dancing to the music of gales and cyclones, to rage against and penetrate this resistance.

So it felt surprise to discover something breaking through from the other side. The surfaces tensed with lines of force, cracking like fractured rocks and, finally, ceding to the pressure of filaments unfurling in every direction. They divided first into hundreds of branches, then thousands, interwoven sinews that trembled upon contact with the air. They grew slowly, arching close to the ground at first, then ascended in an intricate, flexible, fibrous scaffold. It tried to tear them apart with blizzards and squalls, but it handled the gusts as easily as its own soldiers had scattered across that celestial rock. The more violently it tried to destroy this viscous, cancerous network, the more it split and spread wider, climbing above the terrain and filling the space where previously its multiple body had dominated. Each of its embraces was rejected more firmly than the last, and when it finally acceded to reality, mesh-like networks born from these domes held sway over the landscape. Its greed to consume became an obsession, a stubborn frenzy, a meteorologic surge of planetary proportions. But the silent networks extended, unstoppable. Finally, its strength was waning and its army of grains weakening just as those insolent brocades were covering prairies and hills.

As it watched, they rose in towers covered with something like scales or feathers and cast down shadows. These new vegetating structures filled the areas where before it had dominated, massive systems of fabric with palpitating fibers. And it felt its own organism shrink and its strength extinguished. It understood too late that these strange and evasive creatures had been feeding on its energy, integrating each soldier of its army, recombining molecules to transform the inert into the organic.

Its breath slowed and its hunger diminished, and the virulent craving that had harried its senses for so long as its constant companion and merciless torturer began to dissipate. When the urge disappeared with its dying breath, it finally found happiness.

ZERO

THE END of the world caught up to him with death in his throat, running against the wind. Objects flew past him, and a roar engulfed his surroundings like a wound in reality.

He had to keep moving forward.

The dust obscured his sight more than a few meters ahead, but the curb of the sidewalk at his feet meant he was headed in the right direction. Although he was a hefty man, at times he had to grab a light pole or kiosk so a gust would not blow him down as he fought against an invisible fury sweeping everything away.

He had to reach his destination.

He calculated that a couple of blocks of buildings and an empty field remained between himself and the entrance to the subway. Dirt had blown up his nose and into his eyes despite his eyeglasses. He could taste it, damp and pasty, in his mouth, and had to turn his back to the wind to cough. Like a desperado in a cowboy movie, he pulled a kerchief from a jacket pocket and tied it to cover his face.

To his right he could make out the entrance to city hall, its windows broken and interior filled with the same dust that had inundated the entire city. He kept going, not pausing when his path crossed with the few other travelers, most of them letting the wind push them toward the coast with what few possessions they could carry—families, hand in hand, toting bags and backpacks that seemed buoyed by the wind at their backs. He saw lone souls attempting to protect themselves from the savagely dislodged soil and dust. Some walked aimlessly, some lay collapsed on the sidewalk, and a few sat on the curb as if they were waiting for a bus.

For days, no vehicle had traveled the streets. Dust clogged the motors, and people had no choice but to walk.

None of them had anywhere to go.

The ones who left their homes knew they had no alternative: even if they tried to flee the city, the grit-filled monster would continue sweeping away everything it touched, pulling down trees and roofs, blowing open windows and storefronts, turning over cars, burying train tracks, and howling without respite.

He had to fight harder than expected to reach his destination. It was a subway entrance blocked by concrete pylons and a wire fence, construction that would never be finished. Many people had tried to escape the windstorm by hiding in the tunnels. Hundreds of underground kilometers were now home to those who couldn't or wouldn't escape the city, an underworld few dared to leave to look for provisions.

He had been living there for some time after the storm became intolerable and dust slipped indoors through chinks and cracks when life on the surface became unsustainable.

"Hey, Doc! Do you have anything for asthma? My wife can't breathe."

"Doctor! I think my mother is having a heart attack!"

"My baby isn't breathing! He stopped breathing! Do something!"

Death had been at their throats, down in their lungs and hearts. And everyone had called to him looking for a cure, a solution, a scrap of hope.

"We've run out of supplies for inhalers."

"If she has a pulse and can breathe, you'll have to wait for now. Your mother isn't a priority patient."

"I'm afraid your baby is dead."

With every answer, he felt complicit with death. He understood it wasn't his fault, none of it was; he hadn't filled the air with dust and grime and straw and dirt and sand and pebbles. But that certainty did not make him feel better or even less bad. Instead, it left him with a bitter sense of incompetence, as if he had thrown all those years dedicated to medicine out the window, for they could not help him offer care to those who needed it or even ease their pain.

Each time the faces were thinner and ashier in that underground limbo, hands more grasping, eyes more desperate, and with them, more death. He attended a childbirth where the baby had been born dead and the body and placenta, placed at the feet of the mother, had suddenly disappeared, and that was when he began walking deeper into the tunnels, horrified by the dehumanization of people living in the shadows. It felt as if darkness engulfed all living things trying to survive, stripping from them any trace of empathy, as if brutality was the only possible answer to so much suffering.

The electric grid had failed days ago. He roamed blindly through the galleries, guided by the silent rails, sleeping in abandoned subway cars, discarding his few remaining provisions, trying to avoid the people who warmed themselves around fires at the stations.

Day and dusk became confused: everything turned into a permanent state of night at its darkest before dawn. His only companions were the paws of rats chafing on the waterlogged floor of the tunnels, the light of his lantern, which he tried to conserve as much as possible, the voices of those who ventured into that tangle of passageways, and his memories.

Darkness served as a blank canvas where his mind could envision his earlier life, when nights followed days and clouds covered the sun, when it rained and even snowed. Life flourished on the face of the Earth, and people laughed, fought, blasphemed, sang, and could wander through streets and gardens untrammeled by dust. When breathing wasn't a constant challenge, when the air smelled of flowers and gasoline exhaust, when someone could be soaked to their skin in a summer storm and joke about it, when life was in apparent peace, even if fragile and at times uncomfortable.

He remembered long, boring hours spent studying, the smell of fried chicken and salt in his parents' house, the bustle of the student dorm, the unending shifts in the hospital, the call that convinced him to join the Department of Advanced Genetic Engineering, the afternoons in the riverside cafés with his beloved Imogen, the failed experiments, the darkness that began to eat at the days, and the diseases advancing like a virus in a healthy organism.

Then he wasn't sure if he had really chosen to go below ground, or if it had been the other way around.

The move was progressive as he tried to avoid staying too long down under. There was something treacherous in the shafts and corridors, something that made people sweat while their stomachs churned: the feeling of pure greed. It was real, so tangible. Every time he saw a glimpse of good intentions in a person, someone else appeared and washed away hope. For that reason, he opted to return to the surface, even though that meant dealing again with the monster storm. It felt as if he was diving into the depths of some viscous dark liquid and, to catch his breath, he needed to resurface. Had people always been monsters after all?

As a healthcare professional, he was committed to preserving life and, despite the shortage of medical supplies or proper staff, what hindered his efforts the most was society's lack of empathy. Every day the storm rumbled, more people left their loved ones behind, no matter what their relationship, regardless of how they scraped by. He saw abandoned children, elders, sick family members, and pets as often on the surface as below. More people started to drift away without a purpose, just waiting for death to strike them sooner rather than later, baring their bodies to the elements.

For a moment, he thought he could stay sane underground, but doubts invaded him as soon as he hit the sewers. Was he becoming one of those bleak souls he tried to avoid? It seemed impossible to maintain sanity in such conditions, when everybody was fighting for the same resources, when death spread, and madness seized all.

The wail of a child pulled him out of his thoughts. He had encountered few families and the children generally stayed quiet, weakened by hunger and the lack of sunlight. When he heard no other voices and the weeping continued, he drew near a half-ruined subway station where groups of people surrounded several fires. In the group closest to the mouth of the tunnel, bundled shapes huddled together, and the smallest bundle cried unattended. He approached with his hands in the air to show he had no weapons.

"Hello. What's the problem with the child? I'm a doctor, maybe I can help."

One of the bigger bundles turned toward him.

"What child? If you mean the brat, her belly's ached for days."

"Yeah, she hasn't eaten in who knows how long," another voice said from the shadows.

The doctor came closer and touched the child's forehead. She had a fever.

"How long has she been sick?"

"A couple of days."

He gently took the little girl's hand and had her lie on the ground. She was around ten or eleven years old, her face grimy with soot. He palpated her belly as she groaned.

"It's appendicitis," he said as he helped her up. "She needs immediate surgery, or it could become peritonitis."

"Operate? Seriously? We don't even have any food."

He couldn't tell which bulk was speaking or note any movement or gesture to show a relationship with the girl as if no one cared what happened to her.

He looked with infinite sorrow at the little girl's dirty face, greasy hair, and eyes half-shut by fever. It was the same face he had seen on other bodies, young and old, men and women: the face of coming death, the same eyes with nothing to see, the same mouth that would never open again to eat.

He calculated that in her state, she would suffer an agonizing death when the appendix burst from infection. It would have been a simple surgery, just minutes in the right conditions. He wouldn't even need a surgical suite, only a few clean sheets, water, and alcohol to knock her out and disinfect the instruments in his backpack. Without that, there was no hope at all.

He returned to the tunnel, and he thought he heard a choking cry from the little girl behind him, then the sounds of struggle.

He began to run to escape the bundled shapes, the hunger, the horror.

Run.

Inhabiting his own private nightmare and bereft of any means to wake up, he kept running until the feeling of small needles pricking his ribs stopped him, out of breath.

Nothing made sense anymore, so what was he running toward? There was no place safe, nowhere he could hide from the cruelty unleashed by scarcity. With a bit of luck – actually, with a lot of it – he could last a couple of weeks before falling into the hands of desperate drifters. Nobody had anything to lose, and the world was lawless.

It's not as if he failed to resist by every means he could in the very beginning, long before falling into subterranean existence, but each of his attempts to organize people around their new reality crumbled. He could not blame anybody; it was tiring to navigate the chaos of failing institutions, incompetent bureaucrats, and shortsighted authorities. Too much time was lost in fruitless discussions but, finally, a plan for relief was set in place: they were going to break the city into self-sufficient units, each containing a limited area, only a few streets. Each unit would shelter people in indoor facilities: malls, stadiums, concert halls, train stations, hangars, schools, and any other sufficiently large structure.

For a few weeks, things seemed to be working as each person undertook their task seriously--some tracked down resources, some chose to guard their campsites and minimal possessions, while most tried to stay relevant in a world where white-collar work was, suddenly, unimportant. They faced many struggles but surmounted them, one problem after the next. He almost believed they would succeed.

Although they were hardly short of ideas, their leaders couldn't tie their shoes and the intelligent ones were unfit for leadership. Available supplies were supposed to be equally distributed but never were. The privileged got the most and the rest starved.

The cold settled among the ones still standing and diseases weakened the most durable souls. There were simply too many problems, and no one could cope anymore. Arguments arose and disputes progressively escalated until violence broke out. Society's moral compass lost its direction completely as aggressions became frequent with the passing of each week, so groups started to thin out and loners multiplied. At that point, he had no choice but to wander on his own.

Then, time ran out.

A few times he tried once more to gather people

together. A few times he entertained the idea of building a group strong enough to take care of its members. On every occasion, selfishness imposed itself and disaster followed. He lost faith in humanity after the first murder he witnessed, so he decided to return to life in the tunnels and subways. He finally lost faith in himself when he found himself rummaging through a corpse's possessions after spending days without a bite. It was like med school again, disengaging himself from any feelings toward the dead, rationalizing an impossible situation with a mix of victimization and detachment.

The darkness swallowed him again, but footsteps ran toward him, and with them, a light.

"Hey, you're a doctor, right?"

"Who wants to know?"

He immediately regretted his answer. He couldn't face another death. It was simply too much to endure. All he wanted was to be finished with it all. At least, he would decide when and how to end it. Anything would be better than becoming enslaved and tortured. Anything would be better than finding himself enslaving and torturing someone else.

Being a monster didn't scare him. What was destroying him was the *feeling* that he would willingly become a monster.

The light came from an oil lamp. The man carrying it spoke fast.

"It's important."

"Everything seems to be, and really, now nothing is ..."

"Sir, I told you it was. Did you work in a hospital in the city?"

"I was a surgeon at the university, but a while ago I quit to do research. You came too late. There's no way to operate."

"Operate? What're you talking about?" The man with the lamp now stood in front of him in the middle of a gallery at a juncture in the tracks.

"I mean the girl in the station, the one who has appendicitis. Or had it ... I don't think she's alive now."

"Sadly, this place brings out the worst in people ... You said you were doing research?"

There was something strange about the man. His face was ruddy, his clothing worn but not stinking of sweat. He wasn't very thin, either. And, strangest of all, he wasn't armed.

"You don't live down here ..."

The man chuckled, making the lamp shake.

"You're very observant, Doc, but you haven't answered my question."

"I worked in the applied genetics lab at the university."

The man shifted his lamp to the other hand nervously. "Then, do you know Professor Van Buren?"

"Old Van B? Sure. He is ... was ... the head of the department. Do you know him? Are you a researcher, too?"

"No, I'm not, but I know him because we worked for the same organization. Old Van B. limping around everywhere."

The doctor noticed an intention behind the man's words as if he were trying to provoke him. "I think you're talking about someone else. The Van Buren I know is paraplegic." He was turning to leave when the guy grabbed his arm.

"Wait! Do you want to get out of this hole? I bet you do."

He wondered if this was a trap: he'd heard of organized bands that drew in victims to kill and eat them. "Anyone would want to leave this hole. What a question."

"I might be able to help you. But we can't talk here. Follow me. I can take you to Van Buren."

The man gestured to follow him through a branch of the tunnel that led to an upper-level platform.

The doctor hesitated. He had met some staff members of the hospital in the subway, an emergency room doctor, a couple of nurses, a foreign doctor who had been on an exchange program, a guard, and the family of one of the personnel officers, but he had seen no one from the lab where he used to work. He'd imagined that his co-workers had fled the city during the first days of the storm, or that they had simply decided to stay in their homes. This was the first time in a long time he'd heard talk about the lab.

He realized he had little to lose and, no matter what, he could escape into the darkness if things turned ugly.

He let himself be led through a maintenance service door and down several hallways to a mid-sized room with some empty pallets, oil lamps scattered around the floor, and a pile of cardboard boxes against one wall. The place was deserted.

The man with the lamp sat on one of the pallets and pulled the pack off his back.

"Have a seat. This place is safe."

Safe was a concept that had lost its meaning long ago, he thought.

"Where are we?" He dropped onto the nearest mattress.

"In due time. I need to know if I can trust you, and something tells me I can because Van Buren is paraplegic just like you said."

"You were testing me, then."

The man smiled as he took out a cigarette and passed one to the doctor.

"Something like that. I can offer you the chance to

live a lot better. There'll be food, water, and dust-free air."

The doctor studied him uneasily as he lit his cigarette with the light that the other man offered.

"Why? What do you want from me?"

The man took out a canteen and offered it. "Go on, drink. It's potable water, I promise."

He took the container and smelled it. Nothing smelled off, an unusual thing these days. The water he had been drinking after the supplies ran out came from rain that had seeped through the walls and tasted like dirt. He took a long drink, and it had almost no flavor.

"Where did you get it? There's no water like it anymore."

The guy gestured for him to keep drinking. "The place where I'm from has a lot of it. If you come with us, you'll have everything you need, and you won't go hungry anymore."

He drank until his thirst was sated. "Why me?"

"We need people like you, who know what you know, people who worked on Van Buren's team. When you know where we are, you'll understand better. I promise you won't regret it. But we don't have much time. The storm's getting worse and soon staying up top will be impossible."

"Since when does the word of a desperate man matter?"

The man took a deep puff of his cigarette. "Do you mean me or you? Look at me. I'm not desperate. I eat three meals a day, I sleep in a nice bed, I breathe clean air, I fuck when I can ..."

"How did you get a place like that? And why does no one know about it?"

"It's sad that we can't take in everyone. That's why we have to be choosy about who we ask. Life is cruel ... but it's wonderful, too, don't you think? You'll get answers to all your questions. You just have to get where I'll tell you to go."

The cigarette tasted marvelous.

The man showed him the exact location of the entrance he'd have to reach. On a map, he pointed out where they were and the distance he'd have to travel. The problem was that the doctor would have to go outside because the tunnels that should have connected to that stop had never been finished, so there was no way to get there underground.

"You're not coming with me?" He watched the guy fold the map and shove it in his backpack.

"No. I've got to find more people and some supplies. I'll meet you there soon. You can keep the canteen, you're going to need it. When you get there, show it to them and they'll know I sent you."

There was just enough time to finish the cigarette.

Then the man, whose name he hadn't asked, went with him to the door to the tunnel.

"Listen up: only you can go. If you try to take someone else, or if you share this with any of the gangs down here, you'll regret it. We've got good protection. And you'd waste your only chance to live."

They separated there, in the belly of the underground labyrinth.

That was the last time the doctor saw him.

It wasn't easy to travel up and outside. A lot of the platforms on the way were held by groups that demanded a price to get past them. He had to turn back into the tunnels several times until he found an exit where he earned passage by splinting the leg of a gang leader.

The worst came when he was captured by a gang of body snatchers. They made him perform a vivisection on an old lady so they could devour one of her organs, keeping her alive to preserve her body for future meals. With a pistol against his ribs, they forced him to first cut out her tongue so they wouldn't have to hear her howl curses at them. He was haunted by the eyes of the woman looking at him in horror and the smell of her tongue being cooked even as he was cutting open the side of her body to extract her spleen.

He escaped by random, undeserved luck. Another gang followed the scent of roasting meat and burst in while he finished closing the incision. The wordless laments of the woman still tortured him, especially because he didn't have time to mercifully take her life. All he could do was run as fast and as far as possible, hiding from everybody, not just to avoid being captured again but because he felt incapable of facing any other human being.

Maybe this was his own personal hell unfolding before him.

Outside, the wind still carried away everything it could. The streets were filled with a thick haze that he knew wasn't fog but grit blowing in the furious wind. He would have to get through several kilometers of it to reach the entrance. He hesitated for a minute. He could barely breathe, and the air was full of static electricity, like moments before a thunderstorm.

He took another drink from the canteen and hung it on his back before he started off. He found himself wandering through deserted streets again, empty of people but full of dust and sand everywhere. The wind shrieked through the ghost town. He fashioned earplugs with some fabric to block the din, but they only muffled the sound. The piercing constant lamentation saturated his existence and flooded every cell, driving him insane.

Painfully, he arrived at his destination.

The entrance to the subway under construction sat

a hundred meters from the last buildings, and he had to fight with all his strength against the wind as it stubbornly tried to push him back.

As soon as he touched the cement blocks that covered the entrance, he circled to the left, following the instructions from the guy with the lamp, and found a metal door. As instructed, he knocked fast—for so long that he lost track of time. He was about to give up, cursing his fate and wondering how he could possibly get back when he heard the screech of rusted hinges.

The door opened a few centimeters wide. Panicked that it might close, he snatched the canteen from his back and shoved it into the space between the door and the jamb.

"This is what the man gave me who told me to come. I'm a doctor."

The door opened a bit more, barely enough to let his bony, tired body inside.

"Come in before this whirlwind takes you away," a voice said from the depths of a clear green shadow inside.

And he went in.

ONE

HE OPENED his new eyes for the first time. The intense light made him close them immediately. The pain reminded him that now he needed to wear tinted glasses.

"My boy, you're even uglier than before! I don't think you're going to be asked to dance anymore ... or maybe you would. I mean, who knows what the hell girls like these days. You like girls, right?"

The patient tried to sigh but couldn't through his overlapping lips. He raised his hand to separate them and open his mouth, something he'd have to learn to do by moving the new muscles on both sides of his jaw.

"Damn that wind!" the voice said. "It keeps making me nervous every time it blows that hard."

He found it hard to answer. "I don't hear anything, Doctor." At least his voice still sounded like it used to.

"One of these days, the membranes will fly away, Kirmen. Remember what I'm saying. The wind will carry us wherever it wants. I only hope it'll be some-place silent."

The teenager rolled over in his hospital bed. "Have I been asleep for a long time?"

"Several sandstorms."

"Where are my parents?"

"I suppose they're getting everybody's best wishes. I've never seen a couple that can fake being together that well. I almost believed that they love each other. Who knows? Maybe this mission really does bring them together. I wouldn't be surprised. I've seen stranger things."

"When can I go home?"

"You need to let your body get accustomed to this configuration. Close your mouth, boy, I can see all the way to the roots of your teeth!"

"If I close it, I can't talk."

"Why do you want to talk? There's no one here you can give a speech to. Your parents are busy managing your newfound popularity. They won't be back for a while. They'll bring glasses so you can use your eyes. Until then, you'll have to put up with me."

The young man closed his lips and waited patiently. Fortunately, the old man stayed quiet until the ward nurse brought the glasses, then left without a word.

"Do you want me to put them on you or can you do it yourself?" he heard.

"I helped design them. I think I know what to do."

The first thing he could make out when he opened his eyes was the old man, wearing a sterile suit, sitting on a chair next to his bed, scratching the inside of his thigh with evident pleasure. His back grew more bent year after year, and his gray mustache contrasted with his entirely white hair, which had thinned at the crown. The long fingers of the hand that wasn't entertaining itself scratching his groin were drumming on his thigh, playing an imaginary piano. His face, in earlier times, was charming, but now displayed only wrinkles and a constantly disgusted look.

The doctor was pain: blood and skin extractions, inoculations, medications that gave him diarrhea, nausea that left him prostrate for days. Kirmen hated him with all his strength but feared him even more, just like he feared the whirlwinds outside.

Above him, the transparent ceiling; the curtains that isolated his room from the rest of the clinic let the dome be seen here. Outside, the sandstorm grew worse, the wind gusted more violently, and the structure vibrated as if it were about to take flight. The sand took days to settle after the storm, and the atmosphere outside had been the same color as sweaty gauze for months.

Outside was hell.

To Kirmen, the word *hell* seemed empty. If the world was quickened dust, those millions of particles flew like a living organism engulfing the planet, consuming everything solid they met like a vampire, pulverizing them, making itself bigger and more powerful. The monstrous dust devils had ridden the wind forever, and only people the doctor's age had known a time without storms, a time with clear skies, waves in the sea, plants growing in the plains, forests, fields, and sand only at beaches and deserts. If safety existed solely in the habitats under a half-dozen connected domes, isolated from the exterior, then that was the world and the rest didn't exist.

Hell was *outside* for those born before the domes were sealed shut, the people who entered the Cloister old enough to remember a different world they could compare with the present. Those ancient people talked about fantastical things—water extending a million times farther and deeper than the artificial lakes and tanks of the domes, so enormous that one shore couldn't be seen from the other shore, and the water was filled with all kinds of life. They said the seas contained extraordinary creatures, some as gigantic as the electric generators, capable of destroying a boat dozens of meters long with a slap of their tails. Others had elastic globe-shaped bodies sprouting velvety, sinuous tentacles with suction cups that could asphyxiate an adult with their embrace. Enormous communities of fish moved like a single organism, imitating the furious dust.

They also said that before the storms, forests had grown a thousand times bigger than the wetlands in the domes, kilometer after kilometer of towering trees had loomed over the land, where air plants hung from branches and four-legged animals climbed and moved through the green maze. Stories spread describing settlements built near rivers of crystalline water, where cabins were higher than the Cloister domes, made of concrete like the tunnels, now deserted for years, that had connected to the exterior. Those cabins could hold thousands of people in living spaces one on top of the other with vehicles moving vertically between them.

Some people even described powerful machines to look beyond the skies and other machines with generators that could lift entire crews into the air to visit what was on the other side of the atmosphere, whatever was there.

Most people considered all that as the stuff of legend, realities so far from their own that they had to be the fruits of imagination or age-distorted memories. And, despite the pictures and moving images, despite the books and their illustrations in vivid color, despite the sounds heard on recordings, to Kirmen it seemed impossible that the elderly were referring to the same planet where he lived.

Because he, like everyone else born beneath the domes, knew only the Cloister. Their world was made of interconnected habitats with controlled humidity and temperature, in which strict rules dictated social interactions. Zero waste, sustainability, communal work, and life preservation. Anyone deviating from those principles was corrected.

The boy lowered his eyes as he lifted his hands to see if they were as he remembered, the color and texture of oak trees. And they were, dark brown, covered by rough cork-like skin with lengthwise grooves. His arms, unusually long, hung below his knees and seemed more like branches. Long arms and exceptional height made him look like a young tree.

His hair had disappeared in his infancy during the first stages of treatment, so he usually covered his bald head with a baseball cap. He had a couple of them that had belonged to his father, gifts back when they remained in regular contact. The one on the bedside table to his left had once been dark blue, and the letters NY were still legible. He realized he had never asked his father what those letters meant or how he'd gotten the hat, but it was also true they rarely spoke much now.

Kirmen couldn't recall ever seeing his hands or skin looking any other way, brownish and tough. He'd been told that from a distance, he seemed covered with tattoos, and up close, the tattoos were irregular creases remarkably and strangely resembling the grooves on tree trunks.

He had seen pictures from his infancy when he looked like a baby with smooth tan skin. When other boys' faces filled with pimples from hormones, Kirmen grew little knots along his arms, hands, and upper thighs. At times, odd bulges began to develop, but the doctor carefully removed them.

Those lumps were examined to make sure they weren't cancerous cysts. They often appeared on his body, as he was told, because of his treatments. Still, despite his deformed, strange appearance, he grew like a weed, ironically. He was never ill or had the breathing problems that affected many people in the Cloister, and he was immune to the most common illnesses. His dark skin resisted cuts and bruises, and it healed fast. He stoically withstood the pain as therapy caused changes in his body, along with operations and invasive treatments, but he never fell ill from bacteria or viruses, and his postoperative recovery set records.

The doctor kept the cysts in an aqueous solution and even gave them names: Zoltan, Sync, Manna ... Kirmen found it particularly perverse that they were in clear plastic containers clearly labeled as his cysts. One was especially repugnant. It was in the shape of a penis with swollen glands and its label read: "Pixie: cyst #17 from Kirmen." It had grown on his left arm and, after removing and studying it, the doctor treated it as if it were a sentient creature.

"Look at who's here!" he would say, half-smiling, every time Kirmen came into his office. "I told you that the keratinization of his jaw was getting faster, Pixie ... Pixie, you should see these cells!"

Pixie stood in the center of the doctor's desk so that every patient in his office had it directly before their eyes.

The boy didn't understand why that man, after spending years treating him and following his case attentively since he'd been an infant, humiliated him that way. He didn't understand the little shop of horrors his office had become or his obsession with talking to the phallic cyst as if it could listen. He had the impression that he was merely a scientific possession, a decades-long experiment, something that the doctor found invaluable and, at the same time, despised profoundly, that horrified him just as much as it interested him.

As his body kept changing, the doctor treated him

more scornfully, criticizing what he did, what he said, and even what he didn't say, meddling in every part of his life, monitoring how many hours he slept, policing what he ate down to the smallest nutrients, controlling how much exercise he got every day, whom he passed his free time with, if he urinated more or less than usual, if his father had slept at home, if he dreamed and even what he dreamed about. The doctor was especially obsessed with his dreams and had him write them down in a diary he read every time he saw him. The boy wrote what his friend Jana told him because no matter how hard he tried, he could never remember his dreams.

Kirmen finally confided his feelings to his mother, thinking she'd understand.

"You shouldn't be bothered by that," she said. "Remember that you were picked to save us all. You're the chosen one. Our beacon, our hope. Do you know how many people would give everything to be in your place? My child ... one day you'll leave here, and the wind and inhuman dust storm out there won't be able to stop you. We owe it all to the doctor and don't forget that. Sacrificing a little now means a better life. And you'll be the first."

That made Kirmen feel as small as an ungerminated seed, as small as every time Ania, Milo, Kaitz, or the rest of the children laughed at him.

"Monkey fetus!" they shouted. "Cork tree! Scarecrow! You're so ugly no one dared to be born after you!"

That was a long time ago. It happened on the first day in a school that now stood empty. And back then Jana was already defending him with her unusual voice. Pockets of pus had infected her throat during her infancy and left her with a peculiar voice and the habit of clearing her throat after every sentence.

"Idiots, he's the chosen one!"

The girl started coughing before finishing the sentence.

That made them suddenly quiet.

"A fucking monster, that's what he is!" The look from Kaitz, who had shouted that, also had a lot to say. Frustration blazed in his eyes and rancor lay behind the twist of his mouth.

Jana put herself between Kaitz and Kirmen, already a gangly one meter seventy centimeters tall. Despite being short, she didn't seem intimidated.

"You're just jealous, flat face!

Cough.

Kaitz tried to swat her away, but Kirmen's long arm stopped him.

"Don't touch me, monkey fetus!" Instead, he pushed aside the knotty, long arm. "You'll be sorry, you piece of shit and tumors!"

Kirmen never again suffered a direct attack from

the other children, but sometimes rotten lettuce leaves appeared on his desk, his chair reeked after being rubbed by an onion, or caricatures were drawn in his books of an enormous green penis labeled "Pixie" with arms and legs. He could feel Kaitz's hostility at school, his constant challenging gaze, dirty gestures, and the indifference of the rest of the students when it happened, an invisible and constant threat.

Jana and her father Jay were the only ones who treated him as if his skin wasn't miscolored and hard, as if his height was almost a mere accident, as if he didn't look so deformed. He spent all the time he could at Jay's cabin, trying to dispel the bitter sensation that he was an outsider, even in his own room.

"What's it like to be normal?" he asked Jay days later.

The man was weaving a basket from recently cut hemp. They sat on a step of the platform to the cabin where he lived with Jana and her mother.

"To be normal is to be natural."

Kirmen was almost as tall as Jay, who still seemed to be the biggest and strongest man in all the Cloister.

"What is natural?"

The man stopped weaving the basket and glanced at him curiously.

"Have they been rubbing onion on your chair at school again, Kirmen?"

"No," he lied.

"When you lie, you get buds on your nose."

Kirmen put his hand on his nose, and Jay chuckled.

"I knew it! Those kids ... I think I'm going to have to talk to Kaitz's aunt again."

"That will only make him angrier. It will stop for a few days, and then it'll be worse."

Jay put a hand on the boy's shoulder and gave it a hard squeeze. He knew that Kirmen wouldn't feel a simple pat on the back.

"Maybe it would be better to talk to your parents."

The boy shook his head. "You haven't answered my question. What's it like to be natural?"

Jay began weaving the basket again. "Not pretending. Not trying to be different. Feeling comfortable in your own skin."

"I don't even have skin."

The man sighed and looked up. The dome's metal scaffold supported the membrane separating the inside from the outside, keeping it tense and in place. The metal was dark, a special alloy, according to Kirmen's father, highly resistant but with elastic properties to withstand the fury raging on the other side. The bots that maintained the structure were like insects on an immense web guarding them from on high, wheezing as they monitored the tension and patched any tears.

"When those big kids bother you again, think about

how one day you'll be strong, and they'll still be rotting in this hole. Remember that Kirmen."

But there were his hands lying wrinkled and hard at the end of his arms on the white sheet that covered him in the bed at the medical center.

He was studying the fibers and knots on his right hand when a screech sounded through the dome. The curtains around his cubicle ripped open and a woman whose face writhed with pain came in, howling and stumbling as she clutched her belly.

The ward nurse followed, panting behind her face mask. He instinctively put his hand on his ears, but he had no ears. His fingers could only half-cover the ridges and grooves that ran down the sides of his head.

The woman wasn't wearing a sterile suit. Her tunic had a dark stain on the back. She was looking around for something.

She wanted the same thing as the women in the waiting room in the doctor's office years ago, some in their twenties, most in their thirties, and one already in her forties.

He remembered it well because he was the only male there, and, although he'd been in that room too many times to count, the day that he turned fifteen was different. It must have been due to what his mother called maturity, something he'd been gaining over the years, and everyone talked about happily, like a superpower activated by magic after waiting for clues to it from age fourteen.

At fifteen, he should have been used to the looks.

The looks.

Furtive, all of them, and Kirmen usually classified them into two groups: the ones with a tinge of fear, as if they were seeing something malignant, and the ones with clear disgust, like Kaitz and the rest of the kids. Rarely had he seen something different, hostility with hints of envy, and he could count them on the fingers of his roughened hands.

A couple of women wiped away tears that day, although most of them looked sorry. One showed no emotions at all, her impassive eyes fixed on her hands on her lap.

The doctor appeared in the doorway and quickly scanned the waiting room. All the eyes rose to stare at him, except for the emotionless woman. The eyes of the doctor settled on one of them.

"Fatim!"

Fatim stood like a domesticated animal and followed him into the office. Kirmen knew it well. He had been there hundreds of times, a strange place because it had glass windows. Inside the Cloister, solid windows weren't needed because the temperature was constant and pleasant. Only places like laboratories and clinics used them to protect the privacy of the engineers or medical examinations. As if no one knew why all these women came for an exam.

They were all bleeding.

Kirmen caught one showing her bloody rag to another woman, their eyes swollen from crying. She held it as if something precious had broken and she was sad because she had no way to fix it.

Jana had been the next to last child born, and since then, no other had come to term except for him. After that, nothing but bloody rags. There were even rags like that at his house, white linen with reddish stains that could never quite be removed. But his mother wasn't as grief-stricken as the women in the waiting room.

He'd learned about menstruation in school and understood that it was something natural to women's biology, but he didn't understand what caused so much suffering.

"Why do women keep going to the doctor's office, Jana? Do you know?"

She was his best friend, only a few months older than him, and her eyes had stopped being those of a girl several months ago. She didn't answer right away.

"I don't know how to tell you some things, Kir. It's not that I don't want to tell you ... it's something women feel and it's hard to share."

Cough.

Kirmen frowned in disappointment.

"It's a little like what happens with me," she said. "I try but I can't understand what you feel after all the injections and operations. I don't know if you see and feel things like I do, if they have the same effect on you as the rest of us. You're different, and I don't really understand what you're becoming."

The girl almost choked after talking without coughing which, at the end, she could not avoid.

"Don't talk like that. I'm not a monster."

"Did I say you are? Did I? Be fair. I've never treated you bad. Have I treated you different? You don't have the right to talk like that."

Cough.

"Sometimes, the way you look at me ..."

"You're different. A lot. After every operation, you're less like me. You can't expect that, after every change, I can act like nothing happened. We all need a little time."

The conversation ended when Jay, Jana's father, returned from the vegetable fields.

———

HE RECOGNIZED THE WOMAN, SCREAMING WITH all her strength, as one of the ones who came often to the office. She broke free from the nurse's arms and threw herself onto the doctor's chair, almost knocking it over.

"By god, someone bring me a tranquilizer for this woman," he shouted as he struggled with her.

She grabbed the chair, pulling it as if she wanted to drag it around the entire clinic. The old man tried to push her out of it, and the ward nurse tried to pull her out.

In a few seconds, the room was filled with people in sanitary suits. A tall man entered holding a syringe over his head, and everyone turned to look. He cleared a path to the woman. Kirmen assumed he brought a sedative because, shortly after he lost sight of the syringe, the woman stopped howling and began babbling incoherently.

The tall man approached Kirmen's bed and made sure the tubes were properly connected to him.

"How are you feeling, kid?"

He recognized the surgeon and forced his lips open to speak.

"Better, now that I can use my eyes."

"Do the cuticles on the sides bother you? It's normal to feel a little uncomfortable until you can coordinate movements with the eyelids, but that should come with practice."

Behind the surgeon, the woman was taken away,

still murmuring vulgarities. The old man's voice filled the hush she left behind.

"You should file a claim on the guy who left you pregnant, not against me. Maybe his starving little sperm made the pregnancy fail! I've been saying for years that the miscarriages in the Cloister are caused by the environment. Something malignant in this damned place is incompatible with life. When will anyone listen?"

The doctor's yelling made Kirmen remember something about Jana when she was an infant, the only person in the Cloister as young as he was. A watercolor portrait of her as a baby just over a year old hung in the living room of her cabin, something someone had given her parents.

Jana didn't like it. She said that her cheeks were too puffed out, her skin was lifeless, and her eyes were too wide. Jay told her that one of the nurses liked to paint and made portraits of all the babies born in the Cloister. That night, Kirmen asked his mother about that nurse, and her answers were elusive: his mother didn't remember if anyone had asked to paint a picture of him when he was born.

After that, it became an obsession to see if there were baby portraits in the older children's cabins. He spied through the windows when he was sure no one was looking and sometimes managed to enter houses on some pretext. He saw the portraits, and he even caught a glimpse of Kaitz's, ruddy with curls surrounding his face, as Kirmen helped his mother carry in some sackcloth to mend. The picture hung in a bedroom over the smallest bed.

When he was sure that everyone except him had a portrait, he thought about asking the doctor, who always knew everything, had answers to any question, and found out more secrets about the Cloister than anyone. As one of its oldest members, he'd witnessed every important event, and because he'd treated almost everyone, he heard most of the rumors and news in the domes, so he could likely speak with authority.

The doctor's cabin door was closed: the consultations must have finished. He went to the back door, and before he could knock with his rough knuckles, an outburst of laughter made him stop. The doctor had company, which wasn't new, but the collusion in the voices surprised him, a conversation half in jest, half serious, with a lot of laughter, a few sighs, and soon, panting.

The other voice belonged to a woman.

There was something in the timbre, the way she exhaled as she laughed, the soft giggles, the songlike high notes, that became painfully familiar.

The laughter was his mother's.

———

As soon as the surgeon left, the doctor put his face only a few centimeters from Kirmen's. All those wrinkles so close made the boy dizzy.

"Can you smell this?" the old man asked.

"I don't smell anything."

"It would be odd if you did. You don't have a nose, so how would you know that you've peed all over yourself?"

Kirmen sat up and touched the sheets covering him. Despite his corklike, rigid skin, he could feel wetness.

"Shit. How come I didn't notice?"

"Maybe you should lick the sheets..."

"What? That's a sick thing to say!"

"Your sense of smell is now in your extensible lips, so, technically, I'm right. To smell, now you have to suck. I told them keratinizing your penis would have unpredictable consequences, and I'm afraid urinary incontinence might be one of them." The doctor sat down again.

Kirmen looked at the sheets, upset. "This never happened before..."

"You had a catheter. It got pulled out, obviously."

"No one noticed."

"They're all so used to it they couldn't smell fresh shit."

The ward nurse came in with a syringe and injected it into a loop on a green container. The youth showed her the yellow stain on the sheet, and she understood.

When the analgesic began to take effect, she came back with a new set of sheets and tunic for Kirmen. The boy felt embarrassed to change in front of her, but connected to the bags of organic waste, he had no choice.

"How is the woman?" Kirmen asked. "Why did she come in here like that?"

The nurse pulled the stained sheet off the bed before she answered. "The psychiatrist thinks she had a paranoid attack. She's sedated now, and she will be for a while."

The doctor gave the nurse a wicked smile. "Have they done the D&C? She's sleeping like a rock, so it's a good time. It's her own fault. Getting pregnant is reckless. She had it coming."

Kirmen was surprised to hear him talk like that, not by the tone, typical of the old man's rants, but because the doctor had been fighting a battle since the start of the Cloister, a fight against the clock to survive and ensure its continuation. The Cloister was recycling more dead all the time and couldn't keep the birth rate stable.

Every family could tell stories about the miscarriages its women of child-bearing age had suffered. As soon as Kirmen was old enough to understand that the world was the space delimited by the domes, he learned the mystery that worried everyone: the work crews discussed and debated it loudly in the town square. Hours and hours of arguments, testimonies by red-eyed women, men carrying little bundles of cloth with trembling hands to deliver to the doctors. And every month, more bundles, more tears, more trembling hands.

Kirmen remembered the time when he entered puberty clearly because he had suddenly grown to be more than two meters tall, and all his clothing was too small. The boy was convinced that the growth spurt caused his father's absences, which lengthened until he stopped coming home at night, visiting his own home only occasionally. He told his wife and son that the work teams in the laboratory and shops couldn't build enough machines and automatons, and they weren't being repaired and maintained because his staff had to fill in at other jobs due to worker shortages. The youngest residents, including Kirmen and Jana, had their hours cut back at school so they could help in the fields and other jobs, and Jay had to stay late at the workshops.

Jana's father often joked about Cloister claustrophobia, pointing to the line of people at psychiatric services that stretched outside of the building.

One of the immediate consequences was the decision by the medical team to accelerate Kirmen's treatment, taking advantage of imminent hormonal changes. Since then, the injections and surgeries increased. That was five years ago.

———

THE NURSE IGNORED THE DOCTOR AS HE SAID, "If you don't put diapers on him, you're going to be changing the sheets all the time ... Listen, honey! Do you have the hots for the surgeon, too?"

Kirmen's lips, one on top of the other, curved down without him having to move them with his hands.

The nurse worked faster and left dragging the sheets.

"I'd love it if you brought me some tea. Valerian, doll!"

Kirmen felt relieved to be bedridden so he wouldn't have to make it for the doctor. He'd lost track of how many times he'd made the tea, boiling roots and putting up with his bad moods. The doctor had a little garden behind his cabin where he grew medical and exotic plants. Kirmen had asked him once how he got them, but the doctor wouldn't say. Rumor had it he had left the Cloister in its early days, and Kirmen imagined that's where the seeds came from.

The doctor was obsessed with them. They grew in plots around his cabin, they carpeted the roof, and they even clambered on some of the interior walls. Those walls, in a bizarre display, were filled with pictures of all variety of plants and fruits with sketches and notes in the margins, graphs of the life cycles of some specimens, diagrams of dissected flowers, shelves with clear containers of mutated samples, pieces of trunks of various widths hung on fishing line in a corner, and dozens of botany books piled on the desk, sharing spaces with Kirmen's cysts.

The boy would go to the medical center for treatment, but the exams were done at the doctor's house, so he had to visit often. After the tests and dosage adjustments, the doctor had him prepare a teapot of valerian as he spoke of the latest properties he'd discovered in the hybrids he cultivated.

The boy hated those chats almost as much as the needles and knives, which got more invasive every time, but the doctor made him pay attention, claiming it would be useful once the treatment was finished. He made him read aloud pages and pages of specialized books and even learn the strange names of some species, like *Tacca chantieri* or black bat flower, which he'd managed to grow in pots in his office. Kirmen was repelled by the shiny black flowers with dark filaments hanging down like cat whiskers. He didn't like the *Aris-*

tolochiaceae with their bulbous brown flowers that attracted clouds of insects, or the *Hydnoras africanas* that parasitized the roots of nearby plants and attracted its pollinating beetles with a putrid stink. But he did enjoy watching the *Dionaea muscipula*, the Venus flytraps, close their green jaws over flies and small spiders perched on their pretty leaves. The insects fought to escape but soon grew still and were digested by the plant's fluids. The tubular *Sarracenias* grew at the entrance to the cabin, their innocent appearance hiding a big appetite, wafting the scent of nectar to entice dragonflies, bees, and aphids into their slippery tubes. The doctor also cultivated several kinds of orchids in odd shapes and intense colors, with varied bulbs, but he felt a weakness for the *Ophrys apifera*, whose brown and yellow flowers imitated female bees to attract the males as pollinators.

One of his most valued possessions was his reserve of modified *Mesodinium chamaeleon*, one-celled organisms that fed on algae, assimilating the sugar produced by the chloroplasts. The doctor observed these hybrids almost tenderly through a microscope, and he kept complete colonies in test tubes.

Sometimes he ordered Kirmen to accompany him to the warehouse to look for medicinal ingredients or a tank to collect algae to feed to his microscopic monsters, as he called them, fascinated by their single-celled existence straddling the animal and vegetable kingdoms, being one or the other depending on the state of their digestion. He could spend hours studying their life cycle, feeding preferences, and reproductive habits. To the boy, they seemed like simple life forms that responded only to the most basic stimuli, like a change in the alkalinity of their environment or a lack of food. The crude cells, with cilia on their exterior membrane, resembled spasmodic hairy coins.

———

THE MINUTES PASSED, AND NO ONE CAME WITH THE tea, not the nurse or any other staff member.

"What a batch of losers! Would you deny a cup of tea to a poor old man? I taught you everything you know about medicine! I helped you blow your noses when you were toddlers and treated the parasites lodged in your privates when you were teenagers!"

"Doctor, be a little nicer, no matter how anxious you are! No one's going to bring it if you're so grumpy."

"Everything I'm saying is true, boy. In the end, they know I'm right."

"I still don't understand why you're here. Didn't you retire?"

Kirmen wouldn't have missed him. In fact, he was thankful for the heart attack that had made the doctor retire. Kirmen had felt sure the old man wouldn't be seen again in the hospital and would spend his days sitting on the porch of his cabin, surrounded by his plants and strange drawings of vegetables, talking to the cyst in the jar of viscous liquid.

"You'd be surprised to know how much they value experience in a place like the Cloister, an island in the trash heap this planet's become. Besides, this is my project. I designed it. I'm not going to die before I find out how it turns out. These jerkoffs wouldn't be able to do much more than hand out band-aids if it wasn't for me. The idiots would have to fend for themselves!"

"You're always grumpy."

"Should I be happy watching my body rust away like a cheap coffee pot? Old folks have the right to be grumpy, it's all we have left. I've spent years putting up with this damned place and no one cares. All the memories of the battles I had to fight here."

"I don't know why you blame them for their bad luck. You came here of your own free will."

"I've seen fetuses ripped out of their mother's bellies, couples that cut off each others' arms and legs, people hacked to pieces by starving mobs. The Cloister would seem like heaven on earth in comparison, boy, believe me."

Nausea filled Kirmen's throat. "I don't feel well."

"Are you upset by what I remember? You're so

impressionable. You wouldn't have lasted five minutes out there. The first cannibal you met would have made sausage out of you. Do you want to know what a human thigh tastes like?"

The boy was glad that the sedative had kicked in, which made the room grow distant. The doctor faded away as if someone were erasing him piece by piece, and his voice grew fainter with every breath.

TWO

JAY BROUGHT them to the wetland. His hands were made for labor. They were imposing even being mid-sized, but surprisingly delicate when he worked with buds, pruned branches, or planted seeds. He organized farm teams with the military precision of a general. For him, agriculture was a tactical maneuver, not at all meditative, a fight against the elements, the exhaustion of the workers, and the modifications of the plants that sometimes caused unexpected mutations.

They reached the middle of the dome for an improvised picnic among the rice fields: salty crackers, goat cheese, and cold tea. Kirmen sat on a rough bench made of reeds. His feet barely reached the ground, and he swung them back and forth, sucked his thumb, and pointed to the miniature animals around them, calling out their names: he could do more than one thing at once. On the other side of the exterior membranes was a dense haze of sand, not fog. Even at noon, light was dim in the Cloister, although not dim enough to trip the emergency lights.

The three had come from the storage dome, the biggest one of all. The tunnel between the domes had a floor of packed earth and a ramp that ran below the protective membrane that shielded them from the outside. After just a few meters it rose into the dome for growing crops. The walls of the tunnel had been lined recently with modified bioluminescent moss to light the way underground without lanterns. The same kind of moss had colonized the basements of the Cloister. The light, though nebulous and weak, was constant and surrounded their faces with a sickly halo.

Jay described the properties of the modified rice in terms the boy could understand. When his little face looked bored, Jay ran his fingers over his head and tickled him, describing the secrets of managing the biomass and how they chose and prepared new fields to plant. Jay didn't seem to care when the boy paid little attention.

Jana had chosen a lichen-covered rock to sit on, and she swayed back and forth. Jay warned her that if she kept swinging like that, she'd fall, but that only made her sway harder. Her father caught her before she fell back-first onto the ground, and she began to cry.

Kirmen didn't understand her tears since she hadn't been hurt. He only cried if he fell and started bleeding.

Jana, his best friend, kept crying. Kirmen thought that if he had a father like hers, he'd never ever cry. Jana's skin was rosy like Jay's, like everyone's, wholly unlike Kirmen's, already brownish and fibrous, the bark of a young sprout that didn't look like the skin of his friend or any other child. No matter how much anyone insisted he had his father's eyes, he knew that wasn't true.

Jana's sobbing became a cadence that filled the air and little by little joined the sounds from inside and outside of the dome until they became a sort of music.

Kirmen recognized the song: in the background, the base notes, the ceaseless low moan of the wind, an airborne animalistic reclamation of the surface of the land; at mid-distance, the mechanical whisper of the habitat's ventilators, a familiar defiant whir, the sound of life fending off death; closer, the birds, their silhouettes jagged against the membranes darkened here and there where the bots were working inside and out; the water of the irrigation ditches burbling among the rice fields; and the provocative lullaby of genetically modified beings, both plants and animals. Over it were the distant voices of the work crews, shouted orders, shared laughter, and work songs, and in the foreground, the fettered sobs of Jana and the soothing words of Jay.

The tones of all those sounds buffered and stirred each other, major and minor keys linked into melodies, sounds circulating in endless succession, intensities throbbing until they matched the beating of the heart, braided rhythms that could dilute or enrich the emotional states they caressed.

The scene began to fray as if the tones were saturated by a sun that only they sensed. Now there was neither Jay nor Jana, just a collective wail that soaked the final image of cloth hung to dry, with red stains that would never disappear, lines lost at the edges of the scene that became unfocused.

THREE

"THE LIST," murmured the doctor, pulling his hands from his pockets. "Where the hell is it?"

He ransacked his tattered tunic and the fabric tore, allowing a yellow slip to fall to the ground.

"Here," Kirmen said as he picked up the paper.

To the child, it seemed that the seventy-year-old doctor walked more stooped and the wrinkles on his face had multiplied. He, by contrast, was as brown and thin as the bamboo growing in the wetlands. At only ten years old he was already taller than most of the adults.

"Fucked-up pocket," the old man murmured.

They had come to the apothecary, and the woman guarding the door greeted them as she opened it. Like all the storerooms of provisions, the building was always guarded.

The boy tried to associate the names on the list with the blurred labels of the jars resting on the shelves of the room. Each time he found the right ingredient, he handed the container to the doctor. Each time the old man checked the content, opening each jar and sniffing. Then he held the glass close to his nose, trying to read the label.

"Don't forget the valerian root they just harvested."

The boy began to look. "Doctor, why do we prepare the tea? Can't people make their own?"

The man stared at him as he fitted the jar among the rest in his basket. "Oh, they'd like to get their hands into the provisions. But if we let everyone take whatever they wanted, the Cloister would be in chaos."

Kirmen held out another jar to the old man. "It's just tea ..."

"If you let anyone into the apothecary, no matter what, people would begin to medicate themselves, which we have to avoid at all costs."

The basket was full. The boy told the doctor he had finished, puffing through his usual route among the most distant cabinets.

As soon as they left, the guard closed the door with a big latch that Kirmen didn't recall seeing when they'd arrived. The boy, carrying the basket, felt the doctor's hand on his free arm, a sign that they were ready to return.

"Let's go, boy. Move faster because we still have a lot to do before dinner."

Those moments traveling between domes were the only times when the doctor lowered his guard and spoke freely. Walking seemed to activate his mind and loosen memories caught in the corners of the route.

Sometimes he told stories about his childhood when people didn't live in isolated bubbles and the air outside was breathable. Airships rose into the sky and people could travel in them to anywhere on the Earth and visit landscapes different from the ones inside the Cloister. Back then the stars decorated the nights and the cities held millions of people, and they could move unnoticed in them. All that amazed Kirmen, who was used to the same faces crowded into irregular cabins, daily air quality checks, miniaturized animals, and greenery that was sacred and scarce.

What the old man mostly talked about was the pale fear spilled on the planet like milk from an immense pitcher of scarcity, starvation, and death. Then, the vicious wind began to blow.

The times when the doctor recalled incidents from his youth before the wind were as few as the days when they ate fish. Kirmen waited for them anxiously because he could ask questions. The old man's memory was more active in the absence of work. The boy was fascinated by stories of the planet before the disaster when the world was still mostly blue. Then the old man would be carried away by his memories and, best of all, for a day he might forget about treatments.

The child and the doctor passed various structures in the depot dome: grain-filled silos rising from the ground like bubbles; wide barns storing plant fibers, seeds, wool, and leather; warehouses with barred windows crammed with tools, spare parts, and all types of equipment; and tall storerooms where miscellaneous items were meticulously inventoried and kept. Each structure was guarded because they were off-limits for most people. The doctor was one of the few with unlimited access to the facilities, including the under-ground grid of mechanical rooms hosting the Cloister's engines, a place his father, a well-respected engineer, required authorization to visit.

They always took the longest way back, passing through several domed ecosystems before they reached the doctor's cabin, where he saw patients. Kirmen believed the hike gave the man the false sensation of being in a bigger habitat.

Although the tunnel to the left would take them directly to the dome enclosing the town, they entered the one to the right that connected with the factory yard. One of the most popular places in the Cloister, the semi-spherical space contained the majority of its work sites. The boy and the old man passed by the textile mills as the shift changed, and they recognized some of the tired faces emerging from the low-rise buildings. A bit down the road that cut through the space, the open workshops revealed a myriad of craftspeople building and repairing all kinds of objects. Some specialized in housewares, others in construction and structural items, and the rest were dedicated to reproducing or creating miscellaneous things. The crowd was larger than usual: it was an open-doors day and many youngsters were wandering around the trade shops hoping to start an apprenticeship.

Further east, an orange glow announced the still-operating furnaces. Not long ago a pair of them were damaged beyond repair, and since then, the other two active ones worked non-stop. Kirmen hoped they would not encounter forge operators. Their fireproof prostheses and, above all, their modified faces with altered nostrils terrified him. He didn't want to resemble them and yet he was being transformed into something different than the other kids. At least, he thought with relief, there were no metallic-enhanced limbs in his body.

In the right half of the dome, printing halls stood out among the rest of the shops. Around them, the stink of epoxy and glue permeated the air. There, while some workers adjusted the 3D printers' settings to replicate spare parts, others monitored printings already underway. The main problem was the limited supply of base materials, so recycling was not only advised but mandatory.

At the end of the dome, covering almost a third of its surface, the recycling factory awaited them. It wasn't an impressive building by any means: just a hangar with a low ceiling, no exterior walls, and a long and easily jammed conveyor belt. Kirmen knew the place well--everybody in the Cloister learned how to triage from an early age. Many times, he had helped at the funnels directing plastic, metal, cardboard and paper, glass, vegetable fibers, and organic trash to the right modules: metal and glass ended up in the furnaces, plastic and fiber items were treated for further uses, and anything organic became compost. Strict recycling norms were observed in the domes and nothing was wasted.

The hammering sounds and the fumes emanating from the factory yard were left behind when they entered the labyrinthic scientific ward. This dome housed the labs, the test center and research offices, the hospital, and the education facilities, including class-rooms, a library, and a media archive. Kirmen was painfully familiar with many of the facilities either as a student, a patient, or a test subject. He couldn't help shivering while strolling through the paths made of compacted sand--each building held a troubling, even painful memory.

The boy needed to evade the suffering hiding behind doors, crawling in corridors, and awaiting him in corners, so he turned his attention to the old man. Making him talk might help to shake off any invasive feelings.

"Doctor, let's walk ... tell me about old Earth."

The old man kept moving without complying. Kirmen wasn't sure he'd even heard him, engrossed as he was in his thoughts. Perhaps the man just chose not to listen.

Both strolled in silence through the maze of buildings. People acknowledged their presence but only a few greeted them. The boy knew. He sensed furtive glances and subtle scornful faces. Nowhere else in the Cloister were individuals more judgmental than in the scientific ward, as if the more they studied and worked on Kirmen, the less rapport they shared with him.

He was glad they were leaving that habitat behind but was taken aback by the doctor--instead of continuing to the next dome, the old man started to descend the service stairs.

They arrived in a mechanical warren. It was the first time for Kirmen because the doctor had never taken that route in the past. The first thing he noticed was the noise, a loud and familiar humming. Where had he heard that before? It was a strange feeling, although he felt immediately at home in that immense vaulted space crammed with furiously droning machines. As far as the eye could see were wheels of different sizes, compressors, cooling systems, fans, claw poles and boosters, waste treatment devices and hydraulic engines, filters and pumps, and water wheels. Every type of mechanical equipment Kirmen could think of was there. In addition, mechanical workers wearing dirty overalls made rounds cleaning, inspecting, and repairing. Some were sealing joints while others lubricated valves and hinges, controlled hatches, regulated temperature and pression, and cleaned clogs.

"What do you see, boy?"

The doctor's question surprised Kirmen.

"You mean here? Well, there are all sorts of machines."

The man looked impatient.

"You need to pay more attention, boy. What do you *see*?"

The child was confused. More than a simple question, the request sounded like a challenge.

"I see crews working to maintain the machinery."

"You are *seeing* through your eyes. But *seeing* really takes place in the brain. Try harder--you need to think."

More puzzled than before, Kirmen took a long look around him.

"All there is are machines and their operators."

His answer did not satisfy the old man.

"Again, you are using your eyes. *Seeing* is more than describing what you notice in front of you. *Seeing* is making sense of the visual stimuli. Around you, there are not just machines. This is the Cloister's core, where the heart and lungs of our domes reside. What you are *seeing* is life's ins and outs."

Kirmen realized that the noise generated by the machines was strangely like the never-ending gusts from outside that he was accustomed to.

"I wanted you to see the entrails of this hole so you understand how fucked up our situation is. If any of this junk breaks down, we'll all fall into a pit of our own shit."

"My father says that the Cloister has very competent technicians."

The old man leaned on the boy while negotiating a path through the sea of metal.

"Your father was always an optimist. I hate optimists. They are dangerous, Kirmen. When people don't have control, *real* control, over their circumstances, optimism is a luxury no one can afford. And, believe me, we are not in control of our lives. Borrowed time is what we depend on."

The pair found a secondary walkway

bordering the zone where they were and followed it. The old man still used the boy's shoulder for support.

"Kirmen, you need to realize how fragile the Cloister is. How long can we run this place before something vital blows up? Our mechanics, as capable as they are, cannot patch up things forever."

The child wasn't sure of the old man's intentions. They didn't really have any conversations before since theirs was strictly a doctor-patient relationship in which the doctor gave orders and he followed his instructions. He didn't remember any instance in which the man asked him to reflect on anything, much less to ponder their situation under the domes.

"This is it, boy. The monster is waiting outside, and the only thing preventing that fucking thing from sweeping us into oblivion is everything you see here. One day, not far from now, there will be no more spare parts to fix anything anymore. Remember this place."

If the doctor wanted to make Kirmen feel special, he failed. The boy could not make sense of his words and felt anxious. He was starting to get the same awkward feeling as when people treated him as if he was some kind of specimen. Then, he felt blocked and didn't know how to act, the same as he was doing at that moment.

Finally, they arrived at the stairs that brought them to the surface. Then, a sudden temperature change announced the tunnel's connection with the wetland dome. It showed no trace of bioluminescent moss: the arched subterranean roof was lit by swinging emergency lights that could not provide the safety they promised.

The humid air stank even though it was sealed like the other habitat passageways. The odor came from the dome they were approaching with its crops of hemp and terraces of modified rice that needed much less water to grow and gave off less methane than earlier varieties. The shoots in the fields formed a green corridor, while the croaking frogs and buzzing insects broke the silence.

"Please, Doctor. I really want to hear about old Earth. Would you please tell me about it?"

"The memories never come alone. They're always accompanied by bitterness, and today I'm in no mood to welcome them."

Kirmen jumped over a rabbit.

"Is it true that all the fields used to be green?"

The old man paused to pull a kerchief from the back pocket of his tunic and pass it over his neck and forehead.

"There are books and films, boy. I can't tell you anything they don't."

"But they don't tell about the emotions. Tell me what you remember, what it felt like out there. Please."

They had reached a rice field. Kirmen saw Jay's crew working in the fields and a team of technicians measuring the methane levels, both crews ignoring each other.

The doctor paused unexpectedly, his back hunching forward and his eyes closed, and he sat on a rock next to the path. Kirmen watched him for a while, then sat on a nearby rock, too. This was one of his favorite sites in the Cloister, a place he frequented with Jay and Jana, where stares were minimal, and people treated him better. Also, there were many places to hide from everyone else, a particularly preferred pastime for the boy.

A worker from Jay's crew noticed them and came to offer a couple of cups of hot water, looking insistently at the boy. He added some sprigs of valerian to them from the basket.

"When was the last time you saw your father, boy?" The doctor's words cut through the wetland's calm, broken only by the crew's occasional chatter and the drone of the squall outside.

"I don't like to talk about my father."

"I think what you don't like is to be around him. That's not right."

"But you talk to hardly anybody." Kirmen bit his lip.

The doctor nodded and closed his eyes as he held the tea. "I've suffered the curse of this place for years. No one should have to put up with my bile, so I prefer to suffer in solitude, Kirmen. You were born here. You're a child of the Cloister's domes. You're part of a family, one with lots of faults, I admit, but you're all tied together by blood and habit, and I suppose something like affection. Our situations are different. Logically, you look to the future, and I only get visits from the past."

The boy put his cup on the ground. He studied the thought-filled face of the old man, the furrows around his eyes, the rosy spots on his cheeks, and the folds that covered his neck. He looked older, more defeated than ever, and realized that life was silently leaving him like a drip from a leaking container.

The doctor began to stand up.

"Words could never describe how beautiful the valleys were in my childhood. The hills were like green carpets peppered with bright little colored stars, which were the flowers. The breeze from the mountaintops when the snow melted on their peaks was fresh and light. Every meadow rivaled its neighbor in the pattern and shimmer of its green grass."

Still talking, he set his cup down on the rock where

he was sitting, leaned on Kirmen again, and straightened up. The boy noticed that the cup was still full.

"Walking barefoot was a delight, and in the summer, my brothers and I would lie in the shade of the trees. We'd gaze at the foothills of the mountains and watch the goats that ran and jumped across the cliffs like acrobats. Enormous birds glided in the sky through the valleys casting dynamic shadows over us. It was as terrifying as it was magnificent. Sometimes we amused ourselves by running as fast as we could in any direction and stopped when exhaustion overcame us. A person could actually run forever."

They'd reached the area where the bamboo grew. The planting was staggered, varying the age of the cane, so there was always a field of fully grown bamboo to harvest for construction material. The fine, robust stalks rose toward the dome as if they meant to poke holes in it. The tall plants, filtering the scarce light, bathed objects with a suggestive greenish, almost magical ambiance.

They came upon a couple of workers cutting down a small batch, who waved as they went past. The doctor, unlike Kirmen, didn't return the greeting.

He wasn't popular, even though everybody knew the man. Tolerated because of his knowledge and skills, he was only rarely invited to social gatherings or celebrations. In any case, he never attended. While the rest of the Cloister's population socialized at every opportunity, he stubbornly stayed alone, working on his research, looking after his plants, and following Kirmen's progress. The boy asked himself many times why the man acted as if everyone in the Cloister was in debt to him and could not arrive at any satisfying solution. Was he depressed by the forced confinement or was he simply rude by nature? Nothing seemed to drag him out of his self-absorption.

They entered a tunnel that connected the wetland with the next habitat, a temperate forest. They had to pass through a polymer isolation gate that separated the environments to keep the wetland humidity from the forest. Oaks, beeches, elms, arbutus, hickories, and an undergrowth of shrubs and plants produced mushrooms, gooseberries, blackberries, cherries, and a shady environment full of animal sounds. The ground had been organized into artificial hills that gave the terrain a rugged look, with knolls and clearings for meadows. The path that crossed the dome snaked between the trees and shrubs. The sounds of birds, insects, and little animals filled the air, perfumed by vegetation, and saturated by humidity. As always, the wind roared furiously beyond the membranes although, under the dome, not even a subtle breeze was felt, and the air hung still. It was an eerie contrast that the boy was used to, but the old man hated.

Kirmen was amazed the doctor possessed the necessary energy to keep talking.

"My mother told me how my grandmother washed clothes in the river. She filled bags with sheets and clothing and carried them downstream. She had a washboard and stool on her back, and after the laundry was rinsed, my mother would help her hang the sheets over the thickets to dry. Then they'd take out bread still warm because it had been wrapped in heavy linen, and big wedges of cheese perfumed with honey from mountain bees."

The doctor's sudden silence contrasted with the growing chatter of the birds and the brook that burbled next to the path. They walked wordlessly to the pond at the edge of the habitat. The images the old man had conjured felt so alien that the boy could not suppress a sudden shiver. He knew they were possible because the books and documentaries displayed all the same amazing pictures that the man was describing, but often he asked himself if the feelings he tried to evoke were real or just an invention to impress him. Seasons, rain, clouds, or a starry night exploded in his mind like fireworks, and when that happened, he could see himself standing on the old Earth beneath an infinite blue dome.

Before they reached the edge of the habitat, they passed a pair of technicians who monitored the chemical levels in the water. The boy found their white sterile suits strange, since nobody other than the medical personnel wore them.

Again, they were engulfed in the darkness of the tunnel and emerged in the aquadome, the immense gallery that contained dozens of tanks and pools surrounded by an intricate network of pipes. Another work group checked the valves of one of the aquariums where schools of fish swam in different directions. The noise of the filtration motors sang like a distant, unending lament. The doctor leaned on one of the pipes that led from the tank in front of them to the machine room, which infused life into the gallery. His voice seemed to accompany the motorized sob that rang through the dome.

"You have no idea of what the sea was like, boy. Anything I say to describe it wouldn't do it justice, but I'll try … Imagine a space without limits, an immense dome, so immense you couldn't see the protective membrane, a place where the sun would shine without scorching you and where the wind would blow gently, caressing your skin as soft as a fan. Imagine a dark blue surface that extends in all directions, reaching to the far horizon, thousands of times farther than the edge of a dome."

Kirmen tried to picture a world matching what the doctor described but simply could not fathom the proportions. What did it mean--*Thousands of times farther than the edge of a dome?* The distances the doctor was describing seemed monstrous to him. Nobody in their right mind could feel safe in such an unpredictable environment, and yet there was an inexplicable allure to that idea.

No boundaries. No limits.

It sounded dangerous.

And cool.

Some dark spots were climbing toward the top of the curved membrane of the dome. They climbed at the same speed, deliberate and constant, in synchronized lines. That meant the storm had worsened and work to check the protective membrane had begun--the bots were going to do their job.

The boy detested those machines. When they spilled over a dome, they were like black blots that sullied the horizon and brought artificial night to the Cloister. He missed the earthy tone of the air outside, opaque depending on the violence of the winds.

Whenever he saw the bots working, he thought about the ones his father brought home to fix. He recalled the ones with broken hind legs that seemed to limp, programmed to follow each other like a defective pack. He'd resented the ones that followed his father like mechanical shadows, which he talked to as part of routine programming, while the boy felt acute jealousy.

After Kirmen smashed one of them with a rock, a mutual state of indifference with his father was established, and at ten years old, he had already grown expert at it.

Since then, he had detested any tech work and preferred to help in the fields with Jay and the other farmers. Anything to get him away from home. Anything to keep his distance from his father. Instead, he felt at home when his nails were dirty from the soil and his back ached from bending over the crops. He loved the occasional chanting of the crew and the never-ending gossiping, the breaks with lemonade and pita bread, and the lessons about the color of the light required in each growing phase of the plants or when to trim and apply fertilizers.

The doctor stared at nothing, lost in visions only he could see.

"The sea breeze isn't like the gales that threaten us here all the time. They're more like the beat of hundreds of birds. They can gently push a waft of air over the sea. Becalmed, we called it. The horizon is clear blue, although white clouds drift by from time to time. There's no dust in the air, just the smell of salt, seaweed, and water. Imagine millions of aquariums like the ones that surround us ... Can you? That's what the sea is like."

Kirmen watched the banks of fish moving as one.

He tried to imagine a space as immense as the doctor described, but he couldn't. A barrier somewhere kept blocking his vision. In a way, he felt like the fish he saw on the other side of the glass, confined in a space that seemed big, was tricked. They were given the false impression they could go anywhere they wanted. But the feeling didn't bother him despite the doctor's words.

"No words can describe to you what a harbor feels like, boy. The sound of the waves against the docks, the ships' gentle rocking, the light hitting the sails in the early morning, the seagulls guarding the wharves from the sky, and the sailors shouting orders, offering their catch and singing old chanteys. I can still see the regulars lining up at the fish stands, bargaining for better prices, sharing their daily troubles. How can I explain to you the flavor of fresh grilled fish from the harbor stalls?"

"When you talk about those times, you get sad."

As the doctor stood up, despite the background noise, his bones creaked like rusty hinges. Together they continued down the walkway between the tanks.

"I don't feel sad to remember it, Kirmen. I feel sad to know it will never be like that again."

The silence filled the tunnel that took them to the next dome, a mix of heaths and pastures for a couple of herds of modified livestock. Some lambs hurried over as soon as they saw them enter. The doctor had said several times that those animals repulsed him, miniaturized ewes and rams smaller than the lambs of the old days. Kirmen thought big animals would have been monstrous and didn't understand why the old man despised the docile, playful creatures that approached them. The old man shoved them away with trembling hands, but the boy knelt to caress their rosy muzzles.

"You ugly little shits! Get away!"

"Doctor, don't yell or you'll scare them. If you leave them alone, they'll go away on their own."

The path split in two on its way through the grass and heath dotted with occasional trees and rocks. The early nightfall brought on by the deployment of the bots made the herds nervous, unsure if they should go to their corrals or keep grazing. A couple of shepherds brought out lanterns to try to calm them. The outlines of objects began to fade into each other.

The doctor walked faster than usual, making Kirmen almost trot down the path. Some lambs bleated as they passed, then nearby sheep took up the call and began to *baa*. The noise made the doctor hike faster, and the boy noted that the old man was getting out of breath. Although he wished the doctor would slow down, he pressed on with an energy that Kirmen didn't know he had. By then they'd left behind the meadows and were getting closer to the next area, which contained the corrals.

"Let me catch my breath," the doctor said as he leaned on a feeding trough.

The cackling of the chickens from a nearby pen drowned out the honking of the geese swimming in the central pond, all hard to see in the darkness within the dome.

"Those damned critters ... Not even real animals! It's like dozens of pressure cookers whistling at once. At least they could have cloned them to sound like the originals! Roosters don't make such ridiculous noises. Their crowing was majestic, elegant ... not this kind of half-baked laughter. Dammit! Why haven't they turned on the lights? That would shut them up."

"If you want, I could go look for my mother. She's probably around here."

"Your mother has eyes and ears. I'm sure she's noticed ... That reminds me of the time when we were going to see an eclipse of the sun, and we were prepared, carrying sunglasses, waiting for the moment when nighttime would come in the middle of the day. I was very young, not even a kid your age, but even though it was so long ago, I'll always remember how excited people were. My aunt muttered that it was a bad omen and nothing good would come from turning natural time on its head. The streets were filled, a summer day when even the clouds seemed to under-stand that something was going on because they had disappeared. The cicadas suddenly stopped singing and shadows covered the landscape. The dogs barked and ran around confused, and the livestock bleated and stirred in their stables. When the sun was hidden by the moon, it made a majestic halo of fire."

"I've never seen the sun directly, Doctor."

The boy was surprised by the old man's look of disgust and found it hard to interpret his feelings. He didn't understand his reserve, his frequent mood swings, and how sometimes he treated Kirmen like he was the most important being in the Cloister, and at other times like he was repulsive. Often, he believed the doctor sought to provoke him but could not figure out why. It felt as if the old man was picking into his mind, looking for a reaction that never seemed to satisfy him.

Kirmen was about to ask another question when the doctor began to reminisce out loud again:

"I would love to describe the sun to you, boy! But I don't have anything like the right words to do it justice. I can barely recall it myself ... It was so many years ago! It was a constant presence, almost solemn in the sky. It looked like a blazing fire hanging over the landscape, dominating the horizon, insulting the clouds that dared to cover it. It could burn in the summer as if it were trying to punish anything alive. In spring and fall it was like a lover that wrapped its legs around you and gave you sweet, sweet warmth. In winter, we had to guess it was there because it rarely let us see it, and when it did, it was like a fake spot of light that laughed at the way we shivered in the cold. It's a pity you've only seen it in pictures."

Once again, the old man's face displayed a quiet, intimate censure that bewildered the boy.

"The snow, Doctor! Tell me again how it was?"

The doctor seemed to gather strength again.

"But I've told you dozens of times! I've never seen anything more beautiful and menacing at the same time. The snow was as white as the milk from the livestock. It would bite your fingers when you held it, that's how cold it was, and your fingertips would burn when you let it go. It could be hard and compacted or soft and spongy, sometimes ice hard as rocks and sometimes like the foam in the ponds. In the winter the landscape would surrender to the snow and let itself be covered without resistance. Some shapes grew white and rounder than ever, but others turned into icy sharp columns. Nature was anesthetized during the winter months, and the promise of exuberant greenery after it melted kept us hopeful at night. I wish I could describe the way it sounded when we walked on it. It was a long organic crunch that reminded me of crushing rice grains. To walk on the snow, or better through it because often it came up to our knees, was a fight against an immobile tide that left you exhausted. A lot of towns were snowed in when a cold wave hit, and the nights grew long like shadows."

"So, there wasn't snow on the coast?"

"I never saw it, but I think hail might have fallen sometimes. Hail was pebbles of ice that came crashing out of storms. But you'll never see this, not anything like it, and I don't quite know why you want me to keep blabbing about it, boy. People tried before you, and they never got a single memory out of me. Maybe it's because you're the youngest of the lot. You've been the youngest for too long a time. I wonder what will happen to you, to all of you, when the water runs out."

The boy stared at the old man, envying his memories. His body was frail, but his mind was filled with the energy of thousands of generators. So many wonders he had experienced in his life, so many remarkable events he had witnessed, that now his brain vibrated with rich and amazing sensations.

In previous walks, the old man told him about the extraordinary places he had visited in his youth and the different people he encountered. Old Earth was an exceptionally vast space with not thousands but millions of unique individuals and dozens of vastly different cultures. He could listen to him speak for hours about the exotic dishes he tasted on his travels, the local traditions, as well as the many perils he faced.

There was a story about camping at night under the

stars in a distant desert after riding a fantastic animal called a camel. On another occasion, the doctor visited friends in a coastal resort located on a tropical island where coconut trees offered much-needed shade and delicious fruit. There was also the time in which the man got lost in a densely populated city where almost nobody spoke his language and criminals nearly caught him.

The old man spoke about host families in remote places that treated him like an adopted son, about dancing to hypnotic rhythms with thousands of others in clandestine raves, about crossing the ice in a dogsled at freezing temperatures. Majestic waterfalls, prairies stretching on until they were lost on the horizon, streets adorned with colors and music, mountains vomiting fire, and places so high as to erase the blue sky and stop the world.

The doctor's voice had steadily weakened as the meager lights of the stable came on. The familiar glow from the lamps hung outside the building calmed the animals and their grumbling, but the doctor's face stayed hard. It was the grimace of contained ire, a wall of skin and muscle enraged for a reason that the boy didn't understand.

A smiling woman drew near, interrupting their thoughts. Kirmen recognized her footsteps, which he had known since he was small.

"It's good I found you! I was looking for you at the health clinic. I even thought of using a loudspeaker, but the bots had to come out and cover the roofing and we had to turn on the lights. We never have enough energy for everything. Doctor, Sita had another miscarriage. It's the third one this year. She's taking it hard ... very hard. We don't know what to tell her or what to do to calm her down. No one can explain it to her."

"It's this damned place. I've been saying that for years."

"What can we do for her? She's inconsolable. This time she thought her pregnancy would come to term. She followed all your recommendations exactly."

"Sita's strong. She'll get over it like everyone else. Infertility and miscarriages are secondary effects of the Cloister, I'm afraid. That's all I can figure out."

"But Doctor, since Kirmen was born, there are no other children. Women are desperate. Surely something could be done. It's been going on too long."

The old man raised his voice. "Why? For years I've been telling you that it's useless, there won't be any survivors in a generation if we don't adapt. There's no other way out. You want to hold back the tide, and that's impossible."

Kirmen felt odd to hear him speak that way to his mother, one of the few people with whom he maintained contact. She was unconvinced.

"You can't be serious. A lot of women are trying to get pregnant. You've been investigating this longer than anyone, so you must have some intuition, some idea about what's happening in the Cloister."

"We've examined all the women without finding a thing, and there's nothing wrong with the men, either. It isn't organic. It must be the environment--that's the only explanation. It might be that the seal isn't as tight as we think."

Kirmen didn't understand how the doctor justified the babies' deaths without looking for solutions. It was like he'd given up a long time ago.

She blurted out, "But why now?"

"To talk about *now* is to be confused about time. Infertility has been here in the Cloister since the beginning."

Kirmen's mother shook her head and crossed her arms. "But before, babies were born. We used to have a lot of children running around all day and crying at night ..."

"What nights?" the doctor asked. His voice rose above the noise from the corrals. "We've been living for years in half-light. It never ends and it never will and it's like it never had a beginning. I can hardly recall anything anymore and I don't want to. If this boy wasn't so insistent, my memory would sleep. He has the bad habit of asking questions and waiting until I answer, not like the rest of you, always on the go and not letting anyone rummage around until they find something worth remembering."

Kirmen realized that his mother was irate. When she wrung her hands and threw her head back like that, she was seeing red.

"I can't believe what I'm hearing. You know not everyone's ready to make a sacrifice like I did with Kirmen. You know and still you've given up. Aren't you ashamed?"

The boy was surprised. No one talked like that to the doctor. He stood up laboriously, looked at her for a few seconds with contempt, and turned, dragging his feet on the gravel.

Kirmen gave his mother a concerned look, which she returned and gestured for Kirmen to follow the doctor. The boy could not understand why his mother always pushed him closer to the old man. She seemed more concerned about the others, like the woman who had miscarried, than about Kirmen. If he had children, he would never agree to place them under the doctor's care.

He sighed, picked up the basket, and hurried to catch up before the doctor stumbled.

They continued in silence, the boy acting as a guide, asking no questions, and the old man letting himself be guided with nothing to say. They slowly strolled across the livestock habitat contemplating other herds grazing in different pastures. A few herders moved among them, inspecting animals, cleaning their hooves, and examining their teeth. While dwarf donkeys were being guided to their stables, pigmy pigs took pleasure in the mud surrounding the goose and duck ponds. The air was filled with their stink and their cries.

The doctor stopped many times to cover his ears and shout curses at the animals. Several of the livestock handlers gestured for him to go away and one even threw dry cow dung at him. Their responses only made the old man more violent, and Kirmen had to intervene, pulling him back and signaling apologies.

Finally, they entered the tunnel to the dome for the town, which held nothing but cabins of various sizes arranged irregularly to avoid the sensation of an anti-septic plan. The dusty lanes separating the huts narrowed in some places and opened wide elsewhere. All the buildings were just one story tall, built from sturdy reeds, with narrow windows and doors made from hemp fiber.

Some were wide cabins with airy porches and thatched roofs of branches and vines that seemed to invite passers-by to come and sit. Others were small shanties, barely roofed, with a rough hole as an entrance. Wide streets were edged by lawns with trees and well-tended flowers, waterways weaving among the houses, and stone benches at their banks. Smaller streets ended in tumble-down, neglected walls, dirt paths alongside or behind the shanties, and uncared-for spaces without sidewalks.

Not many people were out and about at that time of the day because most were busy working in other domes. Still, a few citizens of the Cloister ran errands or attended to domestic chores. A couple was repairing the roof of their cabin with new fibers. A bit further on, several elderly craftspeople chatted while weaving baskets and crates. A group of loud teenagers played marbles in a clearing.

Some volunteers had been assigned to gather trash with the help of service bots. A crew of climbers was training along the dome's structure while bots were inspecting the outer membrane. At the center of the habitat, in the common square, someone sang a freestyle version of an old love song, and the melody could be heard throughout the entire settlement.

Many times, Kirmen had played, shouting in the middle of that square so everyone could hear it, thanks to the dome's acoustics—a classic Cloister prank, like using hollow bamboo stems to snorkel in the shallow waters of the aquadome, imitating the wind howling, or throwing pebbles at the bots.

The uneven lighting blurred outlines as if the entire

space were drawn from an interrupted dream. They walked past a fountain with a trickle of water. The doctor tugged on Kirmen's arm to indicate that he wanted to rest next to it. The boy helped him sit on the stones edging the pool.

The old man was unusually exhausted, without strength and almost without will. The jars in the basket holding ingredients tinkled when Kirmen put them on the ground, blending with the sound of the water. The doctor raised his hands toward his apprentice.

"Are all the jars there? None were lost? Is the valerian there? Give me the basket."

Kirmen put it on the doctor's lap. "It's all there. I was careful with the basket. The valerian is there with everything else."

The doctor stroked the jars with trembling hands. He took them one by one and tried to read the labels the same way he had in the apothecary.

"We mustn't forget it. We're all upset and nervous. What an awful wind! Let's go make several teapots of it. It's night and everyone can have a cup after dinner. Are you listening?"

"Whatever you say, sir."

"It's very important, boy. Remember, if there's something you ought to remember, it's the power of valerian in this place. Without it, we would have all gone crazy a long time ago."

Kirmen shrugged and tried to reassure the worried old man with a joke. "My mother doesn't like it."

"A stubborn woman. If she'd had some, if she listened to me ..."

The boy looked into the doctor's eyes without understanding. They held a new, unrecognizable emotion.

"I only hope that my effort was worth something, that you're a success. Because you're my legacy. I suppose that this way I feel less broken down, although you remind me of the irony of this situation, the joke that life will never stop playing on me. I don't really need you to remind me that I'm dead, that I've been dead since I shut myself inside this place, that we're all dead, and the only possible future is to adapt to another way of life. I know you don't understand me, no one does ... but don't forget the valerian."

FOUR

THE DOCTOR'S babbling brought Kirmen around.

"You're wilting, boy. And I don't mean metaphorically."

There was no valerian or drying rags, just the room where he was recovering and the old man, close to the bed, taking his pulse with trembling hands.

"You should have let me sleep ..."

"Your parents were here."

He hated the feel of the doctor's hand around his wrist. "They didn't stay?"

"I'm sure they had better things to do than watch you drool. You forgot to close your lips before you were tranquilized, boy."

"I don't feel well."

The doctor looked at him for a few seconds, and dragged his feet, complaining, to the other side of the bed. A V-shaped floor lamp stood next to the wall, and he pulled it to the head of the bed and turned it on. The light was very white, almost blue, although through Kirmen's glasses, it seemed dark green.

The old man stood there, next to his patient, waiting.

The boy didn't know what to make of it. "I suppose I should thank you, Doctor."

Thank.

Thank him.

The mechanism of automatic sentiments.

"You're right. It's the second time I've had to operate. And I have to say that the staff is ghastly. Now do whatever you have to do before you get even paler than you are."

"Synthesize chloro-keratin."

"Whatever you call it! Suck in the light and make scales."

"If I look so bad, I don't know why you stay here watching me."

"I've already told you--you're my project. My project! And we're almost done! I won't give them the pleasure of taking what's mine, what I dedicated my whole life to. Besides, when you're as old as me, what you fight isn't death, it's boredom. You'll give anything to have something to kill time faster. Time is a giant son of a bitch that has us by the balls, did you know that?

When you need it to go fast, it slows down like glue, like a nightmare that won't let you wake up, and when you want it to slow down, so you can enjoy an orgasm like it was a symphony, it hurries up, so you come even before you get to the second movement."

Kirmen began to feel uncomfortable. "Did my parents say when they'll be back?"

"Your mother was ready to wait until you woke up, but your father said he was dead tired and needed to rest. Those were his words, 'dead tired.' As if the weight of the world had fallen on his bony shoulders. Your mother felt dizzy and left to go eat something. I think she'll be back soon."

Ironically, Kirmen felt more distant from his parents than from anyone else in the Cloister. He tried to remember the moment when his family fell apart, and he couldn't. He thought about the words of endearment his mother used and how corrupt they sounded, especially when he compared them to what Jana's mother said. The more devoted Kirmen's mother tried to be, the more the distance between them grew.

Sometimes he wondered if he felt rancor, rejection, or a mixture of both. If only his mother would stop saying how lucky he was to have been chosen! Because he was aware that it hadn't been luck, the only thing he did was be born healthy. Jana's health, on the other hand, had been delicate in her early years, so the protocol couldn't be carried out on her early enough. Kirmen didn't feel lucky, no matter how many times his mother told him that when he complained after every surgical procedure or cycle of injections. He couldn't forgive her for minimizing his suffering. He hadn't chosen this for himself, but his mother had, obviously. She had done it for the good of the Cloister, for the survival of the species, she always said, but only to hide her real reasons.

After he found out about the intimacy between his mother and the doctor, Kirmen began to understand his father's attitude. Did he know his mother had found consolation in someone else's arms? Did he do the same?

Kirmen didn't know why they stayed together. Maybe routine was a more powerful force than the urge for freedom, to love and be loved. Maybe it was part of this thing grownups called being an adult, which made him squirm and feel resigned about turning his back on real feelings and living in a state of emotional anesthesia.

If things had been different, if his father had been present in his life, he probably would have talked with him, told him what he'd found out about his mother's secret visit to the doctor's office, the noises and panting, the way she kept encouraging Kirmen to undergo treatments. But he had left, his absences growing longer and more frequent, and Kirmen concluded that he must know all about it and would rather dedicate his time to his work than to confronting his wife and a son that he could no longer physically recognize.

"Is Jana coming?"

"She's a mistake, boy. You haven't listened. You almost never do."

The doctor meant the way he kept meeting with Jana and trying to keep it a secret because the doctors told them not to. But the doctor knew everything. He even knew about the nights they'd spent together in the wetlands listening to the sounds at night when the storm outside let up. At night, older people said, someone could almost believe that the old world had returned.

Kirmen and Jana had heard talk of the sky and seen pictures that showed a blue canvas hanging high overhead during the day, and bright, tiny lights amid the blackness at night. Lying on the grass, caressing each other, they told fantastic stories about floating machines that could travel long distances in minutes, machines like the cleaning bots but more powerful with wings like the birds that flew in the Cloister. They had pilots and could carry them to distant, exotic lands. At times they dreamed of visiting other domes in far-away places where people spoke different languages and where the food would be different colors and flavors.

Jana's lips tasted like mandarin, and they used to touch his when they still were like lips for a boy of his age, although they were rigid and couldn't feel the pressure. He knew they were kissing because she closed her eyes and held him in her arms, but he already couldn't feel her arms. Sometimes they had let themselves go beyond caresses, beyond kisses, and explored their bodies, but Kirmen's was so gnarled and knotty he didn't dare make love.

Jana wanted to try, but he couldn't stand the idea that he might do her harm, and they wound up in the pond's refreshing water, letting the little fish come close, mutually masturbating until the pleasure exploded: she trembled as if she were cold even as the feeling of heat crossed through her body, and his back arched and he ejaculated a dark green liquid.

He wouldn't let the doctor stain those memories. The old man chewed his words with resentment and made everything he talked about sound muddy, leaving it dirty and debased.

Bathed by the light, Kirmen felt stimulation in the chloro-keratin of his bark-like skin, a sensation so pleasurable it muffled the doctor's words.

He saw himself before immense fields that covered every trace of virgin soil as far as the horizon, which drew light from the earth. Bots patrolled the furrows, detecting and pulling weeds. Their metal shone, not like the rusty, corroded machines in the Cloister. They moved effortlessly, elegantly, precisely and efficiently, in a perfect dance to the rhythm of a silent song.

The air was transparent with barely a breeze, no perennial wind carrying sand, and the sun shone high in the sky, unreachable and stunning for all to see. Kirman raised his hand to protect his eyes and glanced downward. His skin was pink and fine hair covered the back of his other hand. He felt something in his eye and brusquely pulled it out: it was a strand of hair. He passed a hand over his head and sunk his fingers into the hair growing there, stiff and abundant, and he ran his fingers through it with pleasure, noting its texture, playing with the snarls he found, feeling it slide on his fingertips. He recognized it as a memory, the same thing he had done so many times with Jana, fluffing her hair, which she wore short, and which always seemed to resist combing.

He turned to run through the fields in the other direction amid a delightful variety of vegetables surging from the soil. He had no shoes. His heels sank lightly into the dark earth, and the plants tickled his feet. The bigger stalks bent under his weight, and behind him lay a path of trampled grass.

He enjoyed the shade of the towering trees, much grander than the modified ones in the Cloister. Dozens of them spread across the entire countryside, many of them species he could not identify. Their abundant crowns and generous trunks made them look like imposing, motionless creatures with limbs branching in search of the sun as if they wished to embrace it.

He heard the water flowing among the stones of a nearby irrigation ditch and slipped his feet into the current until they felt frigid. He laughed out loud when they went numb, and he avoided the sharp stones on the bed as he waded out.

He noticed dark, shadowy bands crossing the sky and wanted to think they were birds. He watched them, and when he got tired, he looked for a clearing and lay down on the grass.

There was no wind, and that alien thought made him shiver with pleasure and get an erection. He felt the way he did when he heard his parents in bed on the other side of the thin walls of the cabin they shared. His father always assailed violently, and his mother let him, sighing: he fucked with rage, and she with resignation. That would happen after weeks had passed by without his father's presence because he had left for work before the morning siren sounded and often didn't return home even to sleep. His mother used to complain that he was married to his bots, drones, and automatons, just after they finished, and then Kirmen heard him laugh, defeated. Each time he felt less excitement because his parents fucked less often.

Once he had longed for the days when his father still had an engineering lab. Because he was still very young then, the treatments left many fewer visible marks, and he could explore the shelves full of circuits, cables, gearboxes, and chassis. Meanwhile, his father would work, cleaning the guts of some cleaning bot or adjusting the sensors of the drones that ventured out to the exterior, but he also had some prehistoric androids with their entrails in the air. One in particular repulsed Kirmen: a pet-bot in the shape of a rodent programmed to follow his father around the lab and workshops so that, as soon as he entered, it would detect his presence and scamper immediately to his side. Once his father adjusted it to follow Kirmen. He tried to lose it among the shelves and big worktables, scurrying between the legs of the other engineers and workers, while the pet-bot followed him relentlessly.

Those were the times when he and his father spoke the most: his father would explain how the machines worked and the improvements he would make, although most of the plans were mere fantasies. To Kirmen, this seemed like the least boring work in the entire Cloister because he could make things with his hands. Once he asked his father to make him an invention so he could leave, and his father just looked at him with a hard expression that the boy didn't know how to interpret.

But the visits became less frequent, at first because the treatments required Kirmen to spend more time in the clinic or the office, and later, because his father made it known that they didn't have enough hands to fix everything that broke and everything the dust wore out.

Lying on the green grass, he felt the heat of the sun on his skin as he watched the clouds pass overhead, lulled by the burble of the nearby stream and the sounds of animals whose names he didn't know. Then he made up a game and searched for their names, and he felt like a god who bequeathed his creations under an infinite dome.

FIVE

JANA ARRIVED when he felt drunk with energy. She wore a sterile suit and face mask, but he recognized her deep, raspy voice.

"Hello!" The cough that followed made Kirmen return to the room, lying under the light therapy lamps.

"Hello, beautiful! I'm glad to see you!"

Jana was the silent calm after a storm. Although petite and baby-faced, she always wore the expression of someone who had fought with death. She seemed shorter than usual, leaner, her collarbones visible beneath the thin cloth of the suit. Her cheeks had lost their adolescent freshness, her eyes were more sunken, the lips he had adored kissing less fleshy, and her smile seemed worn out from use.

Kirmen had always been fascinated by the air of mystery she projected ever since the day when she came between him and Kaitz. In the Cloister everyone knew everyone else, and it was hard to keep a secret, and yet, although they had been intimate friends for years, she kept something hidden from him that hurt her, that upset her from time to time, and not even Kirmen's sweet good humor could coax it from her.

Once he felt sure she was about to tell him, but at the last moment, her eyes got dark and stormy, like the exterior. Then she became silent for hours, and he didn't know how to bring her out, how to recover the Jana who always won when they counted bots, who was the fastest running through tunnels from dome to dome, who knew all the basements in the Cloister, and who could identify any modified animal after listening for just a few seconds.

"I saw your mother before I came in." She coughed again. "She's spent every operation at your bedside. It's ironic that just when you wake up, she's not here."

"More visitors!" the doctor said. "It's about time to wake up and get moving. For such a famous fellow, not a lot of people come to see you. This deserves a little music to celebrate."

His voice surprised Kirmen, who didn't recall hearing him for a while. He thought he'd left, but there he was, sipping from a cup of tea—loudly as if he meant to substitute the sound of slurps for words. He had turned on a sound machine that hung on his chest. Wagner, his favorite, joined the party.

"Someone shares this room with you?" She coughed. "Oh, it's the doctor."

"We don't share it. I don't know what he does here. He's retired, but for some reason they let him keep coming."

"At least he's someone to chat with." Cough. "Well ... I was trying to look at the bright side."

The young man pushed aside the bracket that held the lamps. "Did you come alone?"

"If you mean Jay, he didn't come. It's harvest time. You know how my father thinks: the boss should be the first to come and the last to leave." A torrent of coughs.

Kirmen felt glad that his lips were extended so he wouldn't show his disappointment. He was dying for news about Jay and the work crew, but Jana didn't like to talk about her father. The boy wondered how the only person in the Cloister who couldn't stand Jay was his own daughter. Her mother would joke that the rift between the father and daughter reflected the weather outside--when there was a storm and the wind scoured the land, they would argue over trifles.

The last time he mentioned it, she spent days not speaking to him. He didn't want to make her angry, so he chose to avoid the issue.

He gently lowered her mask and stroked her chin.

"You don't need to wear this. A while ago someone was so upset they tore up the isolation membranes, and now no one wears protection."

Jana took off the mask and cap that covered her uncombed hair. "What happened?" *Cough.*

"The usual," the doctor grumbled from the corner. "Boy and girl meet, they get it on in every corner ... or, I should say, everywhere they can be alone in this hole. The girl gets pregnant. Then, in this case, she loses the baby. Sounds familiar?"

"You're as charming as ever." Another cough.

The old man laughed. Drops of the tea he was drinking spewed out between the holes left by missing teeth. "They all die here. When was the last time a baby was born?"

"Don't let him get to you, Jana. He's been trying to annoy me since I woke up."

"I'm too old to shut up. Old age is fucking liberating ..."

She smiled. "Grandpa is in a real bad mood."

The doctor leaned forward in his chair, supporting himself by his elbows, turned up the music, spread his legs, and began to fondle himself.

"Do you like it when I touch myself down here? I know you do. Come, let grandpa play with you."

Jana slowly approached the doctor. She leaned over him and moved his hand aside from his crotch and spent a few seconds massaging him, smiling like a naughty girl. The old man groaned with pleasure, then she closed her fist as hard as she could.

"Let's play! Young women? Do they put out for you? Maybe you prefer little girls. I bet you do. With your dirty, perverted mind, I bet you've ruined a life or two. Did you take advantage of them while you worked? Did you? Tell me that you're hot for them. Fess up and I'll let go."

Cough.

The Wagner symphony blared.

Kirmen wondered if the sedative combined with the light therapy was making him see things. He thought about calling the nurse, but something inside wanted to know what would happen next.

"Shit! My prostate!"

Jana kept her grip on the doctor's crotch, and he grabbed the armrests of his chair and twisted them like a beheaded lizard.

"Tell the truth, dirty old man! You're a real sicko!"

She kept her grip even when she coughed.

Kirmen thought he was losing his mind. If this was an overdose, the old man's yelling seemed real enough, but his sweet, timid girlfriend had become strange and vengeful.

He was going to get up when he noticed that the old man had stopped shouting. He had stuck out his tongue and was licking his lips with pleasure despite Jana's grip. At that, she let go and scuffled away until her back was against the wall facing the chair.

"You wrecked my cock. *Auugh,* I like it. I love it! It hurts so good. This wretched old body can still feel something. I think I got hard, and I can't remember the last time."

"You idiot!" Uncontrolled coughing wracked her.

"You act like you're sorry, bitch. I can read your face. I've been a doctor for decades, and I got to see into souls. I bet someone around you was abusing girls."

At that, Kirmen stood up, pulled off the sensors for his vital signs and the needles that connected him to clear plastic bags, and kicked aside the bracket holding the lamps. He rushed to Jana, flattened against the wall.

"Doctor! Shut the fuck up!"

"She might be the victim. Yes! Your father touched you! How long has he made you touch him back?"

Deep, desperate coughing shook Jana's entire body. "Shut up! Shut up!"

SIX

CHEMICAL REACTIONS ARE a dance between basic elements. Variations in their initial states make them join and separate, dance faster or slower, and whirl in pairs or intricate compositions involving multiple participants: reality is an immense choreography.

With the right harmony, precise cadence, proper melody, and requisite tone, the elements arrange themselves into one or another kind of matter. This musical frequency is the soundtrack of reality, and it is what Kirmen hears now above Wagner's electrified symphony and the shouting between the doctor and Jana. He feels his adrenaline change and reconfigure with the chloro-keratin as the elements twirl and leap to the same beat.

The present is becoming the future.

Warm pressure rises from the soles of his feet,

uncontrollably. His scales stand up, his breath distills herbal essences. His hands sting and become as woody as mature shoots, and his skin hardens thicker and becomes bark. Each knot turns into a bud. His vision clouds and although he opens and closes his eyelids and lateral cuticles, he can't stop what's happening: changes continue, seen or not.

What he perceives becomes more granular and vibrates with the longitude of the waves impinging on objects. Reality resembles a painting made with short, fierce strokes, palpating pixels that turn the scene into organic photographs trembling, contracting, and dilating to the rhythm of a strange cadence.

But Jana has stopped coughing. Her eyes, whose lids he has kissed a thousand times, now see something that terrifies her, wide open, although he is so close. Kirmen can't see himself in her pupils and pulls her toward him. He wants to protect her, keep her from pain, drive away the terror transforming her face.

Tighter and tighter, he tries to save her, to shield her so no one and nothing hurts her, but the frequencies fill his mind with such strength he can't hear her begging, hear her skull crack, hear her last breath when she is now a jumble of bones.

The last thing he hears is the doctor.

"Grow and multiply, my boy!"

He now understands who his father really is, and

the indifference of the man who he thought was. The old man's endless speeches make sense as the sight of him fades, and his mother's words disappear from his memory as fast as he recalls them. He now identifies the complicit looks and the visits, gestures, and situations he couldn't understand. He realizes, reviews, and revives them with prodigious clarity before they blur into the air saturated by the flow of oozing resin.

He knows what he is, nameless because he is the first to be it, because no word exists or will exist that he can say, no one can name it or utter it, and even if they could, they would never perfectly capture the sounds and their combination. But that thought disappears like the others. Now he does not need to *think*, only to *feel*. Feelings have no memories because he does not need them. And he who has consciousness but not self-consciousness needs no memories because no difference separates *self* and the world.

Because the frequencies are there, have always been there, hidden within atoms, patiently waiting for freedom, and now they cry out as they stretch from the deepest matter, breaking bonds and making new ones, finding links, building resistance, strengthening, and growing, giving themselves to the only thing worth doing now, which is not to hide from the storm but to seek it out.

And grow.

Reproduce.

And keep growing.

Because to survive he must not hide but adapt.

Roots burst from what were once his feet and sink into the soil, hungry. They seek the depths, carving long tunnels toward the earth's center, which they know as their womb. The salty tang of minerals awakens a limitless thirst, a need to soak up all the moisture in the subsoil, to absorb all the phosphates layered within, to grow and stretch and occupy all the space that remains protected from the hurricanes above.

Branches open between the scales to possess the space, probing for any exit above. They spread with the majesty of the wings of a bird, hardening their trunks, unfurling shoots in all directions, replicating themselves in the proliferation of their buds. They conquer the heights, meter after meter, letting stems, twigs, and buds open like hands for thousands of leaves.

Sap and chlorophyll run through channels that had been red, and thoughts disappear in the depths of a humanlike trunk. Green liquid fills him inside with a pleasant warmth, a sense of fullness and health.

He is now bound to the soil. This feeling, far from frightening him, frees him. Nothing can harm him if the soil is on his side, if he is sure of his own place, an anchorage that extends into the subterranean world full of roots and small animals. He feels moving forms close around him, silhouettes that scramble in gusts in different amplitudes of waves. He perceives vibrations near him, movements in the air emitted in a way he cannot comprehend. He feels no pain, instead, the pleasure of fluids running through his branching stems.

Photosynthesis cycles come one after another, tissues stabilize, and growth accelerates stimulated by an exotic rhythm coming from his depth, a subterranean polyphony with areal breaths arranged in furtive but resounding chords.

New buds surge, stems widen, new leaves appear, and they reclaim the old animal fibers above ground: the object is to flourish and continue reclaiming space.

Vertical growth halts completely, and horizontal growth soon after: they cannot seem to pass a barrier; they cannot grow. He fights with all the force of his wide trunk, sending up shoots to scratch the obstacle tirelessly. His keratin structure, fortified by elements rising from the ground, pushes against the barrier—until it cedes.

The air is neither transparent nor pleasant. It blows in all directions. Light barely penetrates between the grains of sand in the wind, but each ray amplifies his growth. The vegetation at his edges protects the central buds that capture more electromagnetic radiation and form increasingly resistant vegetative skeletons, hundreds of meters of shoots that hold twigs with leaves ever more robust, stems more firm. Flowers unfold, at first timidly, but then surer.

He grows despite a wind continuously trying to bend him, but he concedes not a single centimeter and rises, seeking heights, dominating the airspace, covering his trunks with tough, strong bark that will not be overcome.

He is not alone. Inside he feels a familiar frequency that reaches out through the buds flourishing on his finest twigs.

It sways with him as more light appears higher up, leaving behind the winds that abuse everything they chafe, useless against his wood skeleton. He caresses this inner being with soft new tendrils and awaits it in the intimacy of the innermost whorls of flowers. They exchange fluids with the ease that creates a symbiosis, stimuli that move them simultaneously, and together they let themselves be rocked by gusts of wind.

Somewhere in a stem, hundreds of cycles later, far from the outermost buds still covered by membranes, wrapped by languid vines and branches, one of the strains has matured. It starts to move to the rhythm of a heartbeat.

ABOUT THE AUTHOR

Cristina Jurado (@dnazproject on social media) is a bilingual sci-fi author, editor, and translator. In 2019 she became the first female writer to win the Best Novel Ignotus Award (Spain's Hugo) for *Bionautas* (2021, Literup). Her recent fiction includes the novella *CloroFilia* (2022, Cerebra), the novel *Del Naranja al Azul* (2021, Literup), and her collections of stories: *Mil Desiertos* (2022, Eolas), and *Alphaland* (2018, Nevsky Books). Since 2015 she has run the Spanish multi-awarded magazine *SuperSonic*.In 2020, she was recipient of Europe's Best SF Promoter Award. Her works have been translated into Romanian, Italian, Chinese and Japanese, and have appeared in *Clarkesworld*, *Apex Magazine*, and *Strange Horizons*, among other venues.

ABOUT THE TRANSLATOR

Sue Burke's most recent science fiction novel is *Dual Memory*, coming in May 2023. She also wrote *Semosis, Interference,* and *Immunity Index,* along with short stories, poems, and essays. As a result of living overseas, she's also a literary translator, working from Spanish into English, for such writers as Angélica Gorodischer, Sofía Rhei, and Cristina Jurado. She's currently enjoying life in Chicago.

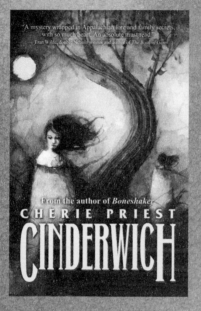

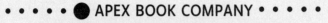
 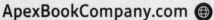